BLOOD ON THE MOUNTAIN

A Western Adventure

A.T. BUTLER

CONTENTS

CHAPTER ONE

"Your deal?" Jacob Payne asked as he tossed his cards into the middle of the poker table. This had never been his game, and he was tempted to just get up and leave, but he couldn't resist trying one more time. He, Edwin, and two strangers had been playing for a couple hours already and Jacob was still running just about even. One more hand—just one more, he kept telling himself—could let him walk away with some real cash.

"Yep," Edwin responded, pulling all the cards toward him.

"This is my last hand," Jacob announced.

There was a short lull while Edwin gathered the deck to shuffle, but no sooner had Jacob breathed a sigh of relief that none of the men were ribbing him for being done than one of the strangers, the one with the mustache, brought up his complaint again.

"Look, I'm just sayin' . . . them Mormons should stay with their own kind."

"They're not hurting you," Jacob said for what felt like the fortieth time. "The man and his family have a homestead miles away from here, aren't coming to bother you or preach to you. What under the canopy is the actual problem?"

"It's just not right," the man said. He leaned his chair back on just the rear legs so he could reach the spittoon. His gob of yellowy-brown saliva fell about an inch short and dribbled down the outside of the metal container. "He's got five wives, I heard. And each one of 'em has a passel of kids. It ain't right."

"Now, how does that work, exactly?" Edwin asked with a grin. "Do the wives all sleep in the same bed? Do they have different rooms? Or do they each get their own house and the fella has to move between each one?"

The mustached stranger—Jacob thought his name was Abe—grimaced. "I don't know," he insisted. "It ain't my business."

"Did you even meet the man?" Jacob asked.

Abe was speechless for only a moment

before spluttering, "I didn't need to *meet* him to know. I heard. And it's not right."

Jacob sighed. It was impossible to argue with someone who didn't have any actual point. "You about ready for that next hand?" he asked Edwin.

The dealer grinned and nodded.

The other stranger had remained silent this whole time, but at least his aim with tobacco was better. Jacob eyed him surreptitiously as they played. Abe had called the silent one Lucky, but there was no telling if that was the name he always went by or just one of several different aliases.

As a bounty hunter, Jacob had to keep his suspicions always at the forefront, not taking anything at face value, as though sinister possibilities were everywhere. Because in Jacob Payne's experience, they were.

Either way, the nickname seemed apt. Lucky had quietly added to his cash over the evening. Jacob didn't always mind losing, but he didn't like seeing one man win that big and that consistently. It took all the fun out of the game.

But he kept his mouth shut.

As the cards landed in front of him, Jacob gently lifted up the corner to see what he had been dealt: four of spades, jack of diamonds, three of clubs, nine of diamonds, seven of hearts.

He kept a close eye on the others as they placed their bets. Lucky seemed confident—maybe that's where his luck came from—but Jacob hadn't been playing with them long enough to be able to read any signs of what kinds of cards they may have in front of them.

It went around again and Jacob drew three new cards, keeping his diamonds but not getting anything new worth a damn. Jacob looked at his dwindling cash and reached a decision. Besides, he didn't want to stick around and listen to more of Abe's griping.

"That's it for me," he said, dropping his cards on the table. "This has been a rich evening, boys."

Abe grinned. "C'mon, stay a bit."

"And give you all more of my money? I don't think so." Jacob clapped Edwin on the shoulder as he passed. "I'll see you tomorrow."

"You off to the cafe?" Edwin asked with a wink.

Jacob paused. He hadn't actually put the idea to himself, but as soon as Edwin mentioned it he realized that was exactly where he was heading. Having a drink by himself—or maybe in the company of a certain waitress—

sounded like the perfect way to end his evening.

At Jacob's silence, Edwin laughed and said, "That's what I thought."

"Good night," the bounty hunter said pointedly on his way out the door.

The San Xavier Cafe was only a short block away from the Golden Saddle Saloon where he had been playing. Tucson was growing, and fast. There was even a rumor that they'd get their own newspaper later that fall. Jacob walked purposefully through the dim streets. The sun had just set. The sounds of drinking and the beginnings of evening entertainment surrounded him.

He was getting tired of this heat. All the Arizona locals had warned him. He'd laughed it off. But they were right and he was wrong. His first summer in Arizona had been a shock. When he was on the trail of an outlaw, focused and determined, he could easily ignore the discomfort. On days like this, however, when he was still trying to find a suitable horse to purchase or waiting for a new tip to come in, the heat was all he could think about. It overwhelmed him and influenced every decision.

Thankfully, with the sun now below the horizon, the evening was cooler, if only a little.

Jacob took off his hat as he stepped through the door of the San Xavier Cafe and fanned his face. He spotted an empty seat at the bar, and was sure to catch the waitress's eye as he sat down.

Bonnie Loft made her way across the room to him with a shy smile. Her dark, almost black, straight hair was pulled back off her face in a low bun, but the tiniest wisps had fallen out to frame her face. Every time she unconsciously reached up to push a strand back behind her ear, he couldn't help but smile at the gesture.

"I haven't seen you all day, Jacob," she said, teasing. "Did you not eat today?"

She ran her small hand across the broad expanse of his back as she crossed behind his seat. Her touch was casual and fleeting, but Jacob knew she wasn't friendly like this with all her customers.

The old Irish bartender appeared in front of Jacob with a neat whiskey. "Usual, eh, Payne?"

"Thanks, Mickey."

"It breaks my poor heart to see you drinking such dodgy rubbish."

"I know." He grinned. "One day we'll go back to Dublin and you can show me the real stuff."

Mickey Sheehan was anywhere from fifty to

eighty years old, and spoke with a brogue as thick as molasses. Jacob once heard that the man had been on this continent for going on thirty years, yet still he talked about his home town as if he were going back any day—including how terrible the whiskey was all the way out here on the western side of the continent.

Jacob raised his glass in thanks and took a sip. The warmth that spread through his torso made him feel better about his losses at the saloon. He was improving at poker, though. Maybe tomorrow night he'd try again, if he was still in town.

Bonnie leaned against the bar next to him, watching and waiting for him to be ready to talk. Finally, she said, "Where've you been, Jacob? You've got another bounty to go hunt down?"

"Not yet." He took another small sip and shook his head. "If I had a horse, I could go to Prescott or farther west where there are rumors of cattle rustlers. But in the meantime I just have to wait here for some chance to buy a suitable animal. I'm not used to such limited options."

"There's nothing in town that suits you?"

"I guess I'm just picky. Paint happened

across my path on my way out here from Texas and I couldn't have asked for a better horse. Nothing here in Tucson right now even comes close. Maybe I'm just waiting for another perfect horse to wander into my life."

"It is a shame that man shot him."

"Jed Corker?" Jacob stared down into his drink. He was still angry about that outlaw shooting his horse out from under him. He took a beat to calm his temper. "He deserves everything the law can throw at him."

After a moment, Bonnie rested her fingers lightly on his forearm, drawing his attention to her. "Why don't you take my mare, Jacob? She may not be the perfect companion for you forever, but she's a good horse to borrow for a bit. Lord knows I won't need her desperately for a week or so, and she stays cooped up so much of the time. With Franny you can get out of town."

He mulled over the offer. That might be exactly what he needed. For the last month he had been going nonstop. Now that Deputy Lowry didn't have any immediate leads on any of the wanted men in the area, it might be just the time for him to distract himself from the heat for a bit and scout out options elsewhere.

"That's an idea," he said. "Only question left is where I'd go. Down to Mexico?"

She nodded. "Or what about the White Mountains over to the east? I haven't been there myself, but I hear good things. There's rumors of gold being discovered out there. Maybe you can use that good luck of yours and stumble across a couple nuggets."

Jacob chuckled, thinking of his last poker game. "I don't know about luck. I'd settle for just a horse. And being in the mountains does sound nice."

"You didn't have any real mountains back in Virginia, did you?"

"Not near where I lived, but I passed through the Blue Ridge Mountains on my way out here to Arizona. I do miss the forests of back east." He sighed, remembering the rolling hills and dense forests around his family's Virginia farm. He could spend hours out there, just listening to the sounds of farm life, smelling the pine and the rotting leaves underfoot. But, he reminded himself, he had left that farm for a reason. Arizona was his home for the foreseeable future and now was the perfect chance to see some of what it had to offer —other than parched and desolate desert.

"I almost stayed in the White Mountains

before coming here, you know," Bonnie said. "It's a beautiful place."

Jacob finished the rest of his whiskey in one long gulp. Now that he had a plan, he was ready to get going. But first, he'd need one last night's sleep in a proper bed.

"You've sold me, Bonnie." He set his glass down and waved Mickey away when the older man came to offer him a second. "If you really can spare her for a couple weeks, I'd be glad to take you up on that offer."

"Well, now I don't know if I want to let her go if that means I won't be seeing you for a couple weeks." She leaned close. "I'm teasing, of course. I'll have her ready and saddled for you here tomorrow morning, if that works for you?"

"I couldn't ask for more." He stood up from his stool and suppressed a desire to hug her, holding her petite body close to him. "That means I have a lot to do before tomorrow, so I'll be saying goodnight."

"Goodnight, Jacob." Bonnie wore a wide smile, but her eyes didn't reflect the same joy as she said goodbye to him. Perhaps she wanted to hug him as well.

. . .

By the next morning, Jacob had everything sorted and packed early. He carried it all over to the San Xavier Cafe to meet Bonnie and her mare.

"Is this your girl?" he asked, approaching the gray mottled mare that stood in front of the building.

"Yes, sir. This is Franny." Bonnie fed her horse half of an apple and whispered to her. "She'll be good to you."

"Thanks, Bonnie. I'll bring her back safe and sound in a couple weeks or so."

"You'd better, Jacob Payne. I want you back safe and sound, too."

He kissed her cheek and swung into the saddle. A few days in the mountains, around real, green trees, would refresh him like nothing else could.

CHAPTER TWO

Jacob and Franny began their long trek northeast across the desert. Riding toward the sunrise, Jacob felt a fresh new start, a blank slate, and imagined the wide expanse of possibility before him.

Somehow he had missed passing through the White Mountains in eastern Arizona on his way out west earlier that year. The idea that there was still unexplored wilderness everywhere around him was exhilarating. He might be the first man to spot a particular tributary of a river, or witness a wild predator take down its prey. He could be alone in the wilderness, not seeing another human for hours, if not days. He could leave his mark, without competition, without challengers. After all, wasn't this why men left the cities and civilization on the eastern seaboard? Why, in fact, they crossed the Atlantic Ocean to conquer the new continent centuries ago? The untamed wild of the western territories was just sitting there, waiting to be inhabited. And now Jacob would have a chance to claim another piece of it, if only temporarily.

He wasn't sure where exactly he was headed, but he was sure he'd know when he got there. Between Tucson and the mountains were a number of small towns, both mining and rail-road, and Jacob aimed to stop in as many of them as he came upon. He'd heard that talking to the men of Globe or introducing himself to the small town sheriff usually yielded informa-tion or bounties beyond what most bounty hunters actively sought. Jacob had learned long ago that there were details everywhere if you just paid attention.

Midway through his first day, Jacob rode into a small town of perhaps eight hundred people. The single long main street stretched before him, dry as a bone with dust being kicked up. Men tipped their hats in greeting as he rode past; women smiled at him, welcoming the stranger to town. Jacob thought they must not have had much trouble here if not a single citizen was wary of him.

After making a few inquiries Jacob discovered the town was called Falcon, and he was politely directed to the town livery where he boarded Franny for a few hours. She deserved a nice rest after their long ride, and he could spend the time eating, replenishing his stores, and maybe even resting himself. Jacob was still not used to the idea that he didn't have any outlaws to pursue at this moment. Far more common was a constant alertness, and he had not yet settled in to such a long break.

Another kind soul directed him to the saloon where he could get a drink and a hot meal. As he walked through the door, no fewer than three of the men inside looked up and nodded their hellos. He relaxed the smallest amount as he found a seat and got his food.

As Jacob drained his first beer, an older couple approached his table and introduced themselves. The older man wore a stark white beard, bowler hat, and trim brown suit that reminded Jacob of his father on a Sunday morning. The woman next to him, also with stark white hair under a small hat, hung back half a step, as though used to letting her husband lead the way.

"Good afternoon, sir," the man began, offering his hand for Jacob to shake. "We are so sorry to interrupt your mealtime, but we couldn't help but notice you're a stranger to Falcon."

"I am," Jacob answered cautiously, his relaxation all dried up.

The man gestured to the two empty chairs at the table. "Mind if we sit?"

Jacob nodded.

"My name is John McFadden. I'm the mayor here in Falcon. This is my wife, Constance. What brings you to our humble little town?"

Jacob took a moment to gesture to the bartender for another beer before answering. He tried to hide his smile at the thought that the mayor himself was the personal welcoming committee of this small town.

"I'm just passing through," he said.

"What is it you do, son? Is there anything we can help you with while you're in town? Anyone I can introduce you to?"

"That's very kind of you, Mr. McFadden. But I really am just passing through on my way to the mountains. I'm a bounty hunter by trade—"

Mrs. McFadden interrupted him with a frightened gasp.

"Are you all right, ma'am?"

She seemed unable to speak for a moment.

Her husband cleared his throat. "What was your name, sir?"

"Jacob Payne."

"Mr. Payne," he said, his voice suddenly stern, "we don't want any trouble here. Falcon is a safe, quiet community, and if you're going to be coming into town raising a ruckus, we don't need your kind."

"No, sir." Jacob looked both of his hosts in the eyes. "That's not why I'm here. Quite the opposite. Hunting down an outlaw is serious business, and I treat it as such. I do my duty to capture the renegade and hand him over to the law. On my honor, sir, I have never once had to kill in my line of work. I really am just passing through your town."

She pressed her hand to her bosom, her eyes wide. "Oh, lord, there couldn't possibly be a fugitive here, could there? We've never had such a thing."

He paused before continuing. In his experience, it simply wasn't possible that Falcon would never see trouble, but could he tell her that? Lying was always his last resort, but sometimes it couldn't be helped, especially in order to protect someone. He was always having to weigh his options and judge the lesser of the two evils. Sometimes a little misdirection really was the best option, or sometimes he could sense that they wouldn't hear the truth anyway. Pieces of the truth were often sufficient, and the listener would never need to know what he had held back from them.

"No, ma'am, I'm sure you're perfectly safe here. If you've not had a bank robbery or kidnapping in Falcon, there's no reason to worry."

"Oh, God bless you," she said, exhaling.

He smiled politely and said his goodbyes. Better to get on the road sooner than he had planned than to be roped into another partial truth. He and Franny had plenty more terrain to cover.

The next afternoon, Jacob rode into a town so small he wondered if it even had a name. There appeared to be only two public buildings and half a dozen homes scattered within a three-mile area. He slowed Franny to a casual walk and made his way down the sole street. As he passed one of the two buildings, a rotund man with shaggy gray hair came out into the doorway to greet him.

"You lost, son?" he asked jokingly. "Not

many strangers find their way to Cork, Arizona."

Jacob waved in greeting and nudged Franny toward the storefront. "Is that where I am? Cork? I've come from Tucson on my way to the White Mountains and wasn't sure what I'd find in between."

"Yes, sir. You found us. Tie up that gorgeous creature you're riding and let me get you a drink."

"Mighty nice of you," Jacob replied as he dismounted. There was only a single hitching post on this street, but seeing as Jacob was the only one here, that didn't seem to be a problem.

"Come in, come in," the man said. "My name is Marty Colfax."

As they stepped over the threshold, Jacob recognized the shelves and storage of a general store, the tables and chairs of a diner, and the counter and workroom of a post office. Jacob loved these kinds of small towns, where a single man fulfilled three or four different roles for the residents.

A kind-looking woman with a pile of graying brown hair atop her head waited behind the cash register. A young teenage boy came out of the back room wearing an apron and carrying a towel, staring at Jacob as he entered.

"It's a man," the kid said in awe.

Jacob laughed. "Well, Mr. Colfax, you weren't kidding about not many strangers here, were you?"

"No, sir." He pushed ahead of Jacob farther into the room and offered him one of the tables. "I want to say it's been almost a year since anyone new has come through."

"Thirteen months," the kid whispered.

"Ah, yes. Thank you, professor." He remained standing next to Jacob's table as he gestured to the other two. "This is my family. My wife, Hester, and our youngest, Amos. We have one other older boy, Joel, back at home repairing a fence today. And, I'm sorry, I didn't catch your name."

"Jacob Payne," he replied, removing his hat and nodding politely to the woman and child.

"Mind if I sit, Mr. Payne?"

"Not at all. And please call me Jacob."

"Okay then, Jacob." Colfax sat across from him and leaned over the table on his elbows, suddenly staring hard at him. "Now, we are good Christians and we want to offer hospitality to any man that walks through that door. But at the same time, the world is a wicked place and I need to be sure I'm protecting my own."

Jacob nodded slowly. "I understand."

"So I'm going to need you to tell me exactly what you're doing in this backwoods corner of the territory."

"Of course, sir." Jacob clasped his hands on the table, demonstrably away from his weapons. It was such a stark difference from his welcome in Falcon that he couldn't help but respect this man's boldness. "I'm a bounty hunter."

"Oh heavens," Mrs. Colfax interrupted, clutching her neck. "There's an outlaw in Cork?"

"No, ma'am. I'm sorry to scare you," Jacob said, trying to be soothing.

"Then what is it you're doing here, Mr. Payne?" Colfax asked.

"As a matter of fact, I find myself out here *because* there are no bank robbers or murderers for me to chase. I came from Tucson, as I mentioned, and the U.S. Marshal there is doing such a great job that the tips for wanted men are few and far between. So a friend suggested I get out of town and look to see if I can be helpful elsewhere. I'm told the White Mountains boast of some of the most beautiful forests in this part of the world, so I'm on my way there to do some poking around, check in with the lawmen, and"—he smiled disarmingly —"maybe even get in some fishing."

"Guess there's not much opportunity for fishing in Tucson," Colfax said, finally leaning back in his chair.

"No, sir, there's not."

"So you'll be on your way tomorrow?"

"Yes," Jacob said cautiously. "Unless you'd like me to go now."

"No, that's not necessary. As I said, we're Christians and we'll feed you and give you a roof. I'd like you to turn your revolvers over to me while you're here, if you don't mind. But we have plenty of room in our barn for you and your horse to stay the night."

Jacob paused briefly before responding. "That seems fair, sir." He placed his revolvers on the table, careful to make sure the barrels were not pointed at his host. The bounty hunter slid the weapons over, trusting his life and his defenses to a man he had just met.

In truth, assuming there really was no danger in Cork, this would be a comfortable, relaxing evening for him, and if that meant turning over his weapons for a few hours then he was happy to oblige. In the few months he had been chasing bad men, Jacob had learned that sometimes trusting the good ones was the only way forward.

CHAPTER THREE

Once they made their way to the Colfax homestead, his host showed Jacob to a new barn, clean and warm. With Franny settled in for the night, brushed and watered, Jacob was looking forward to a night of relaxation. He smiled to himself—Bonnie had led him well. So far he'd had no trouble in finding a kind stranger who was willing to help him feel at home.

The two men stood in the doorway of the barn, discussing Jacob's route the next day, farther toward the mountains, and where he could go to best find the fishing he aimed to do. The cool evening breeze wafted across his sweaty brow.

The farmhouse door opened, spilling light

across the ground. Mrs. Colfax crossed the dirt yard from the house, carrying a quilt in her arms. "You will probably need this. The nights get cool around here," she called as she drew closer.

"Thank you kindly, ma'am."

"Will you be staying for breakfast?"

Jacob took the armful of fabric from her when she reached the barn. Before he could answer, they were interrupted by the sound of galloping hooves tearing toward the barn from the darkness.

"Mr. Parr!" Colfax said as the rider drew closer. "What on earth are you doing here at this time of night?"

The horse slowed as it approached the barn, and Jacob noticed the man's saddlebags and supplies seemed to be minimal. Either this man was counting on the kindness of strangers, or he expected a quick journey.

"I've been sent to get word to the U.S. Marshal's office," the man said, panting a little as he climbed down off his horse.

Jacob jumped into action, helping the man bring the exhausted horse inside, remove the saddle, make sure it had water, and take care of the animal as best he could. He heard Marty

Colfax gently suggest to his wife that she return to the house. While Jacob worked, he and Marty asked the man more questions.

"What happened to your telegraph office?" Marty asked. "I would have thought that'd be easier than tearing across the country."

Parr shook his head. "Blasted Pickens cut the wire. We didn't even realize until a couple hours went by with no response. He gave himself a head start."

"Who did?" Jacob asked.

"I think his name is Pickens. Or maybe Picketts? I'm not certain. He weren't in Elk Springs too long."

"That name sound familiar to you?" Colfax asked Jacob.

He searched his memory but shook his head. If this man was wanted for a crime, it wasn't anywhere in the Arizona Territory that he knew of. Or under either one of those names, at least.

"What did he do, Parr?" Colfax asked quietly, checking behind him to be sure his wife had gone.

"One of the Kimball ladies has been kidnapped."

"I'll go," Jacob said resolutely. "I'll find her."

"And who the hell are you?" Parr said, his

voice full of accusation. He seemed to have finally recognized that he had no idea who he had divulged all this information to.

"This man is a bounty hunter," Colfax clarified for his friend. "Let him help."

Parr nodded reluctantly. "All right. If you say so. But trusting strangers is what got us into this mess."

Colfax led them into the house where Mrs. Colfax had already returned and started a pot of coffee. The kitchen table was clear, save for the older boy, Joel, tucked into the corner reading his Bible. He seemed all arms and legs to Jacob, right at that age where his body was still growing but before the mass of muscle had filled in.

"You're fine, son," Marty said when the boy moved to vacate his chair. "You're old enough to hear this."

"Mr. Parr," Jacob began as the men sat. "I need you to tell me everything you know."

Mrs. Colfax placed mugs of coffee in front of each of them and Parr pulled out a flask to add a little something extra to his. He took a sip, shook his head as though clearing the cobwebs from his brain, took a deep breath, and began.

"This man—Pickens, Picketts, whatever—

he showed up in Elk Springs four or five days ago. Not many. Claimed he's from St. Louis and was looking for the rumored Herron Gold Mine. Now, of course, there's no telling if any of that is true. As far as I can tell, he asked around, got friendly with a number of the families, and had everyone just eating out of his hand, easy as you please."

"How many people are in Elk Springs?" Jacob asked.

Mr. Parr thought a moment. "I'd say near five hundred."

"And the men have already formed a posse?"

He grimaced. "When I left, a couple of them were trying. But there aren't many men willing to stick their necks out for the Kimballs."

"Why?" Jacob asked, bewildered.

"Excuse me," Joel said, quietly but firmly interrupting. "Did you say the Kimballs?"

"Yes," Mr. Parr said to the boy. He turned his attention back to Jacob. "The Kimball family is Mormon. That alone makes them a bit queer, but they also live about three miles or so outside of town and don't associate with us regular." He shrugged.

"So, because they worship a bit differently, there are people in Elk Springs willing to let them be kidnapped?" Jacob tried to keep the accusation out of his voice. The poker game of the night before, with that idiot Abe, flashed in his mind.

"Well, now," Parr said defensively, "if it were just a matter of one of them breaking a leg or needing help with the cattle, the people of Elk Springs would jump to help out their neighbor. But rescuing from a devil?"

Mrs. Colfax approached the table with two mugs of steaming hot coffee in each hand, set them gently on the surface, and handed one to each man in turn. Jacob thanked her as he received his, taking a deep whiff of the rich aroma.

"You can't blame them for wanting to stay safe," Colfax said, sipping from his own mug.

"Right." Jacob recognized it was easier to acquiesce even if he didn't agree. "Are there any leads? Any idea where he's gone with the victim?"

"Mr. Kimball says he followed the horse tracks as far as the river, and then lost them. But they were headed north. The same direction as the rumored gold mine."

"When you say 'rumored'—"

"It don't exist," Parr said emphatically. "Half of Elk Springs settled there because they were looking for that mine, and if none of us could find it in the last couple years then it ain't there."

"But does *Pickens* know that?"

"Could be. Could be he wants to look himself. Could be he was just using that as an excuse to talk to the women."

"What happened that made him snap and take the girl?"

Parr shook his head. "I don't know. I didn't have a chance to do no investigating before I came tearing down the mountain. All I know is a young girl like Flora . . ." He trailed off, glancing warily at Joel.

Jacob knew what he was thinking without it having to be said out loud—what they all were thinking. The risk of a girl like that, of any female, in the company of and under the control of a man like that . . . well, in all likelihood, if she lived through the event she'd never be the same.

"You aiming to go after her, Payne?" Colfax asked.

Jacob nodded.

Colfax turned to Parr. "In the morning you can go on to Desierto, where I'm sure they have a telegraph office, but that may be too late for Flora."

"I want to go," Joel said from his corner. Jacob had almost forgotten he was sitting there. "I'm going too."

"Honey, I don't think—" his mother began.

"I have to go, Mother. I have to. It's Flora." The pleading and heartbreak in his voice was unmistakable. "Mr. Payne will find Elk Springs quicker with me to guide him. We can't lose any time."

"Joel," Colfax said, "I don't want you getting yourself tangled up with any outlaw."

"I'm a grown man, Father. And you've said yourself we're Christians who try to do good by our neighbors. If the men in Elk Springs, who all have wives and children to support, won't go, then someone like me should. Flora needs help."

The boy's parents exchanged a glance. Jacob witnessed them have what amounted to a fully silent conversation, just communicating with a twist of an eyebrow and shrug of a shoulder.

"You're right, son," Marty finally said. "If it don't bother Mr. Payne none, your mother and I will consent to you going."

Jacob was torn. He liked to work alone while he was on the trail, not have to be responsible for anyone else. But this boy—this young man—was clearly desperate to accompany him.

He might try following no matter what he's told.

"I can't vouch for your safety, Joel. It will be rough and dangerous. Not only is there a chance we might fail, but there's always a chance we might die. Are your parents prepared for that? Are you?"

Joel closed his Bible and rested it on the table. "I am, sir."

"Well, then." Jacob nodded. "Let's make whatever preparations we can. We'll leave at dawn."

The next day Jacob found himself on Franny, following Joel through the sparse pine trees on the slight incline up the mountains, as the sun came peeking over the horizon. They had left the Colfax homestead still in the predawn dark and made steady progress through the foothills. In spite of the danger of the mission ahead, Jacob was elated to be back among the evergreens.

"It's not much farther," Joel called over his shoulder. "We should get there well before supper, I think."

"How often do you travel to Elk Springs?" Jacob asked.

"Pretty often."

"You know the Kimballs?"

Joel didn't respond initially, but eventually he slowed his horse to walk alongside Jacob's. "Maybe Father didn't mention this last night, but my family used to live in Elk Springs. Amos and me were both born there. We moved down to Cork when I was about fourteen, but I've known Flora Kimball since they got to Elk Springs. Most of our lives, I'd say."

Jacob waited for the boy to say more. He had learned there were some people who just needed space and to be allowed to take their time, rather than pressing them with specific questions.

But he never did. Instead, Joel gave him a pinched smile, flicked his reins, and rode on ahead. Whatever place the girl held in his heart, Joel was keeping her close.

The incline was getting steeper now, the trail more narrow. At times Jacob lost sight of it completely, but Joel seemed to know where they were going. They rode one behind the other, instead of side by side, and stayed quiet, each listening to the forest around them.

After some time, above him Jacob heard a creaking sound. He tried to turn to see what it was, but the mare was skittish at the sound.

"Shhh, it's okay," he said. But in that moment, when Jacob turned his attention to the horse, he missed the five-foot-long branch as it came crashing to the ground just next to them.

Franny bolted.

CHAPTER FOUR

The second the enormous branch crashed to the ground, Bonnie's mare, Franny, tore through the unfamiliar woods at a gallop. Jacob clenched his teeth, but he willed himself to relax into the mare's stride. It had been a long time since a horse of his had spooked. He didn't want to hurt her or scare her more, but he needed to calm the horse and get her back under his control.

Why hadn't Bonnie warned him that her horse was high-strung? He might not have taken her on this journey if he had known. This was the first time he could remember being angry with the woman, but this was the worst thing that could happen. Jacob couldn't be dealing with this, looking after a young man and worrying about the mare when he was hunting down a kidnapper.

Franny wove between the tree trunks, seemingly without destination or thought to how far she was taking her rider away from the trail. Jacob took deep, slow breaths, talking calmly to Franny and letting her lead until he could calm her down. He reached forward to stroke her mane, placing his broad hand on the tense muscles of her neck.

After some time her frantic gallop slowed to a trot, and finally Jacob was able to guide her to stopping altogether. He dismounted and spoke soothingly to Franny, his low voice helping to slow her heart rate. The poor girl was petrified, and even through his frustration he couldn't blame her. He wondered when was the last time she had even seen a tree, let alone had one almost fall on her. It took a few minutes for her to stop trembling, but she seemed to trust Jacob enough to allow herself to be led back through the trees, back toward where they came from.

Jacob was far off the trail now. During Franny's frantic run, he hadn't been paying attention to where they went or what landmarks they passed. He had a pretty good idea, though, and Jacob stepped over fallen branches and through undergrowth toward where he thought Joel might be.

"Hello!" he cried. If he could just get within the boy's hearing, he could easily find the trail. "Joel?"

There was no response, but Jacob kept moving forward, eyes open for any indication of a path to Elk Springs. There would have to be more than one path around here, right? The town wasn't a fortress or stronghold. Somewhere nearby there must be some indication of humans making their mark on the wilderness.

But after twenty minutes of walking through trees, Jacob still didn't see anything familiar. The broken branches and other signs that he might use to track an outlaw weren't enough for him to trust it as a path back to civilization. He thought for sure he would have come upon the trail or the boy by now.

After another five minutes of walking without finding another clue, Jacob finally admitted to himself that he was lost. Deep in the trees as he was, it was difficult to even see where the sun was. But at least he knew that uphill would be east. Or, it *should* be east. Why didn't he think to get more specific directions from Joel? Why hadn't he considered the fact that they might get separated?

"Joel Colfax!" he yelled again.

He wasn't afraid of making noise. After all, the more noise he made the less likely he was to be surprised by a bear or whatever other predators might be in these mountains. Were there bears in Arizona? Mountain lions? There must be. Just another question he should have asked before setting off to some unknown terrain.

Franny kept close to him, nudging at his collar periodically. Maybe she sensed animals outside Jacob's range of sight. Or maybe she just was afraid of another branch falling. Either way, Jacob kept a comforting hand on her as they tried to find the trail again.

He kept moving in the direction he thought was south, along the length of the mountainside rather than farther up or downhill. He was certain that eventually he'd find something that would help him get his bearings.

Jacob took a deep breath, filled his lungs, and yelled as loud as he could. "Hello!"

"Hello?" a tiny voice answered him.

Jacob couldn't be certain where it was coming from so he yelled again. "Joel?"

"Mr. Payne?"

That second response floated down to him from uphill. Jacob's stomach sank as he realized he had been going the wrong direction. If he had not heard the voice at that moment, he may have wandered around the mountainside for hours more.

"Keep yelling, Joel," he called, relieved.

"Hello!"

Joel periodically shouted to Jacob, often enough that the bounty hunter was able to put himself in the right direction, heading uphill toward where the boy waited for him. He continued to lead the horse on foot until they finally reached the trail.

When Joel came within his sight, Jacob noted the tree branch on the path. "Did you just wait here for me?"

The boy nodded. "Is that all right? I thought I probably shouldn't move off the trail in case you came back."

"That's perfect. Let's hope nothing else spooks this girl."

"Yeah." Joel furrowed his brow. "Is she going to be okay?"

"I dunno. She's not my horse, so I'm not sure. I'd hate for her to become a problem on the trail."

"You can't— I mean, um," Joel stammered. "What I'm trying to say, sir, respectfully, is that I'm worried. I can't let anything stop us from rescuing Flora."

"I know, Joel. I'll figure it out." He swung back into the saddle and nudged Franny forward. "Are we close?"

"Yep. Should be. I think only another ten minutes or so."

It was even less time than that before Jacob smelled the distinctive scent of a cooking fire. A couple of them, he thought. That thick smokiness mixed with the delicious aroma of roasting meat guided them. All of a sudden, Jacob realized he was starving. Whatever it was, he couldn't wait to eat it.

The trail leveled out as the trees thinned. The mountain continued to climb ahead of them, with the town of Elk Springs nestled into a small hollow on the mountainside. It wasn't yet sunset, but many of the buildings they passed shone from within with lantern light. The warm, pleasant glow of suppertime welcomed the two travelers.

"We can stop at the tavern," Joel said. "Follow me."

Before they got much farther, though, they were stopped in the middle of the road by a group of men. A tall man led the group. He wore his blond mustache long and unkempt, connected to his sideburns. The man glowered at the newcomers from under his hat as he stalked toward them. The rest of his group followed closely and casually but visibly held their guns. Shotguns, revolvers, and pistols rested in hands ready to pull the trigger if needed.

Jacob reined in Franny, slowing to a stop at Joel's side.

"Joel Colfax?" the mustached man in front asked. "Is that you? What are you doing here? What are you doing with this stranger?" He glared at Jacob, who silently met his gaze.

"Mr. Parr showed up at our place, Sheriff Dale," Joel said. "He told us what happened to Flora. Me and Mr. Payne have come to help."

"Mr. Payne, huh?" the man asked, still glaring at Jacob.

"That's right," he said. "Jacob Payne."

The sheriff walked closer to them, and Jacob silently willed Franny to stay calm and not get spooked again. "What makes you think we want your help?"

"I'm a bounty hunter and have some experience tracking down wanted men. I'm happy to help if I can."

The man looked skeptical, but was interrupted when one of the others in the group spoke up. "Let's get these fellas fed, anyway, Chester. They musta had a long ride from Cork.

We'll fill Mr. Payne in on the situation and then he can decide if he still wants to help."

Jacob tried to get a sign from Joel about what he thought, but the boy was trembling with fury. Clearly something in this short exchange had upset him greatly.

"That's mighty kind of you," Jacob answered for both of them.

Just a few minutes later, Jacob found his horse safely boarded in the Elk Springs livery and Joel and himself seated at a long table in the Elk Springs Tavern, surrounded by the armed welcoming committee.

"Dig in, boys," said the sheriff. "I know you been on the road all day."

Jacob gladly took his first bite. The smoked elk and potatoes were warm and satisfying after following its smell on their approach up the mountain. He took a few more filling bites before he broke the silence with his questions.

"Could you men fill us in on what has been done to rescue Miss Kimball? What are we dealing with and what do we already know?"

"*Miss* Kimball." The man on the end snorted with suppressed laughter.

"Is that funny?" Jacob asked.

"It's Mrs. Kimball," the man called Chester clarified. He was seated directly across the table from Jacob and Joel. He had been called sheriff earlier, and seemed to be the leader of this party.

"I'm sorry." Jacob looked from one man's face to the other. "I just assumed she was a daughter, since she's younger than Joel."

"She *is* the daughter," Joel said emphatically.

"I don't know about that," Chester said condescendingly. "Those Mormons are known for taking more than one wife. Why else would this Kimball fellow live way out in the wild like he does, if he were living like normal folk?"

"What?" Joel spluttered angrily. "What are you talking about? I've known the Kimballs since I was five years old. They are exactly like you and me."

"That may be, son, but that don't mean you know the whole truth."

"He doesn't know what he's talking about," Joel said to Jacob. "Flora and her sister, Edith, their mother died when they were young. The new Mrs. Kimball is their stepmother. Not their sister-wife or whatever they're called."

"Do you know why they live so far away from the rest of the town?" Jacob asked. He had to admit that did seem suspicious. Living so far away from help and supplies was a big risk. There must be a reason for it.

"Wouldn't you if you had to live with such closed-minded, un-Christian pigs like these?" Joel gestured to the man sitting opposite, clearly not caring that the man could hear every word and criticism thrown his way.

"Boy," the sheriff said, "you watch your tone. Maybe she is Kimball's daughter. But those folks are real queer, and we don't know he didn't take her as a wife, too."

Many of the other men at the table shifted in their seats, shooting looks to each other and shaking their heads. Jacob felt the room shift, away from the sheriff, distancing him and his ideas from the rest of the group. Jacob suspected that they were willing to follow him if it meant not having to go after an outlaw, but they still couldn't hold with calling their neighbor names.

"Now, Chester." The same man who had soothed him earlier spoke up. "That's a mighty strong accusation. Let's not speak ill of our neighbor without any kind of proof."

"I don't need proof. I can tell."

"You don't know anything," Joel said coldly. "Flora Kimball is kind and pure, and at this very moment she is in the clutches of a madman. We have to go after her."

"We'll not be going in the dark, though,"

Jacob reminded him. "So let's get back to the discussion of what has been done and what you boys already know."

There was a perceptible pause while all in attendance waited to see if Chester wanted to speak. When he continued to shovel food into his mouth angrily, the man to his right spoke up.

CHAPTER FIVE

"We haven't actually gone after her at all," the man said quietly, looking down at his plate. He quickly took a bite, filling his mouth with food so he couldn't be expected to say more.

"What?" Joel said, aghast. "I thought— I mean, Mr. Parr came tearing into Cork yesterday. He made it sound like you were treating this as an emergency. What have you been doing all day?"

"We are treating it as an emergency. That is, we did. To the extent that we contacted the U.S. Marshal."

Jacob almost wondered if he had misheard the man. He looked from one man to another, trying to ascertain exactly what he was dealing with, who was calling the shots, and how much help he could expect from them going forward. To their credit, all of the men aside from the sheriff seemed at least a little embarrassed by their lack of action. Staying safe and comfortable was one thing; acting cowardly was quite another.

"Start at the beginning," he said firmly.

When no one spoke up, Joel prompted, "Mr. Parr told us that this man showed up a few days ago asking about the Herron Gold Mine?"

Each of the six men traded glances. Jacob thought he felt one of them kicking another under the table, but still no one spoke up. Three of the men took large bites of their meal and averted their eyes. Without specific details of the girl's kidnapping and what information the outlaw might be working with, Jacob despaired of finding her easily. He looked from one Elk Springs man to another, waiting for one of them to step up and volunteer details.

Sheriff Dale finally acquiesced, but only to volunteer another man. "Arnie, you're the first one who talked to him. You tell Mr. Payne about what he said to you."

The cluster of men looked at the thin, gangly young man at the corner of the table.

Jacob followed their gaze expectantly, trying to hide his impatience. Arnie put his fork down and pushed his plate away from him. He took a deep breath.

"Yeah, so—" He cleared his throat. "This Pickens character showed up here a few days ago. We get some strangers in town from time to time, since Elk Springs is the biggest place on the mountain. He came into my store, asking for rope, a pick axe, and some other things. I think I musta been the first person to talk to him. While he picked out the supplies he needed, he made small talk about the rumored mine, like most strangers do. I didn't think anything more about it.

"I think I told him everything I know. I wasn't in Elk Springs at the peak of the mine-searching, but I know some of the history. I, um . . ." He looked at the sheriff, who nodded his encouragement. "I gave Pickens the names of Kimball and Colfax, who, to my understanding, had searched for the mine the most."

Joel gasped and started coughing, as though choking on a bite. Jacob pounded on his back a couple times before the boy could gasp out, "You gave him my father's name?"

Arnie nodded apologetically. "You have to

understand, I didn't mean no harm by it. Your father ain't even 'round here no more. I thought this man was just like every other would-be miner come through here searching after a dream. I couldn't help him, but I could send him on his way."

Joel's anger could be felt like a wave coming off of him, so Jacob interrupted with another question, lest the boy start yelling.

"That was the last time you saw him?"

"No, not exactly. Over the next two or three days we saw him go in the saloon, the livery, make small talk with the women who came into town to do their own shopping. He sent a telegram to someone in Santa Fe, then hovered in the office for another couple hours, eaves-dropping and asking questions.

"He must've gotten the name Kimball from a couple people, not just me, because yesterday morning he went out to their place. It's a good three miles or so out of town. He definitely went there looking for something particular."

"And you've talked to Mr. Kimball about this?" Jacob asked.

"I'm getting to that," Arnie said, holding his hands up to ward off any further questions.

The bearded man sitting next to him

jumped in. "Yesterday, just before lunchtime, Kimball himself comes tearing into town yelling for help and riding straight to the sheriff's office." He looked pointedly at Dale. "He was hollering about Flora getting kidnapped."

"And then you all formed a posse and went after her, right?" Joel looked anxiously from one face to another. "You went after her right away, right? Tell me you started immediately. She's only seventeen."

Arnie shook his head, looking embarrassed. "You gotta understand, none of us know Flora. Kimball only ever comes into town by himself and leaves the rest of his family out on the property. Boyd here has glimpsed a few of Kimball's women from afar, when they're out in the garden and he rides out to check trap lines."

Joel's fury was growing. "What does that have to do with anything? Even if you didn't know her, she still needs your help. Why would you not give your neighbor whatever aid you can? Isn't that the Christian thing to do?"

There was an awkward silence as each of the men avoided meeting the eyes of either Joel or Jacob. A heavy silence had fallen over the group. Jacob noticed one of the men fidgeting with the buttons on his vest, another flicking nonexistent dust from his hat.

They were hiding something. Jacob needed to know what it was.

He began quietly, trying to keep the accusation out of his voice. "I suspect there's something different about the Kimballs, some reason for hesitation from a community that would otherwise do everything they can."

"There's nothing different about them," Joel protested. "They're the most honorable family I know."

The silence persisted, until the sheriff happened to peek up and catch Jacob's eye. He fixed on the man an expression of such determination that he finally spoke.

"Well." He cleared his throat and sat up straighter. "You see. Reverend Fowler had the idea that maybe the girl being kidnapped was a judgment on Kimball for taking multiple wives."

"What?" Joel shouted.

Jacob put his hand on the boy's shoulder to keep him from leaping completely out of his seat and knocking over the table.

"We didn't want to go against the Lord's will," Sheriff Dale muttered by way of explanation.

Jacob glanced at the young man next to him. It looked as though Joel had been shocked into silence. He sat gaping, open-mouthed, at the group of men sitting around him. He had been so well trained to respect his elders, he didn't appear to even know how to react when faced with such a situation.

For Jacob's part, he had found that keeping his temper usually led to more cooperation from whoever he was angry with. But in this situation it was a struggle.

"I see," he said. "And this Reverend Fowler knows the Kimballs well? And you all trust him to show you the will of God in this?"

"He is a man of God," Sheriff Dale said indignantly. "Who are we to doubt him?"

"The reverend does know the Kimballs," Boyd clarified. "He rides out to their place maybe once a week to try to preach and show them the true way of the Lord."

"He goes out of his way to make that family feel shamed?" Jacob clarified.

"If he really knew them," Joel muttered, "he'd know that Flora is Mr. Kimball's daughter."

"Well, maybe he's done taken a daughter as a wife," the sheriff retorted. "Those folks're known to disregard all of the laws of both God and man."

"He wouldn't," Joel said. "He would never. They would never. Mr. Kimball is a good man."

"How long has it been since you lived here, boy?" the sheriff asked. "A lot can happen given enough time."

"I know Mr. Kimball better than any of you. He helped my family and treated me like a son when I was little. And I was just there visiting less than a year ago."

"And during that year," Dale persisted, "maybe he took his daughter as his wife. Or maybe he done something else. We don't know. The Lord works in mysterious ways, and you'll notice it was none of our daughters been kidnapped."

"I think we're losing the thread," Jacob said, taking control of the situation again. "Setting aside the reverend for a moment, let's go back to when Mr. Kimball came riding into town."

The sheriff sat up straight, confident in his part of the story. "He came straight to jail, told me what happened, and rode home again. Claimed he needed to make sure the rest of his family stayed safe in case Pickens came back."

"And that's when you consulted with Reverend Fowler?"

He nodded. "He advised that we not risk

any other lives on behalf of the sinners, so we don't draw God's judgment on ourselves."

Jacob barely resisted rolling his eyes.

"We didn't ignore it completely, though," the short, stocky man on the end said. "We sent for help."

"True," the sheriff said with a nod. "We sent a wire to Tucson. She had been gone for a couple hours already, but we didn't want there to be any blowback from the law. We did our part. It wasn't until a couple hours later when Mrs. Merrill insisted she was still expecting a wire from her sister in Kansas City that we suspected the communications weren't going through. Sure enough, Boyd here climbed atop the telegraph office to investigate and found the wires cut."

"It took you all day to notice your wire had been cut?" Joel asked.

Jacob marveled that the once quiet and respectful boy was now taking these men to task.

Dale held his hands up defensively. "Well, now, hold on, Joel. Elk Springs is not a busy place. Sometimes we go days without using that machine. There's no way to know exactly when he made the cut, but we suspect Pickens probably did it just before he took the girl.

"So, then, Parr left to get word to the lawmen and . . ." He trailed off. "And then the next day you two showed up."

Joel groaned and leaned forward, resting his forehead on the unfinished wooden table.

CHAPTER SIX

Jacob nodded, his mind racing at all the things he had to do to clean up this mess the men of Elk Springs had created—or at least let fester by doing less than nothing. He didn't say anything, but sat up and continued to eat, putting forkfuls in his mouth and thinking while every man at the table watched him for a reaction.

The first thing they needed to do was figure out where Pickens might have taken the girl. And why. Why Flora? He assumed she was an attractive young woman, given Joel's seeming devotion, which could be reason enough for a man like Pickens to kidnap her. He didn't want to think about what that meant for Flora's prospects, including her chances of survival. He would deal with that later. Once she had been found.

The next thing they had to do—and Jacob groaned inwardly at this realization—was find a different horse for him to borrow. Franny would have been perfectly fine for a few days away from town, but Jacob was no longer on that track. The poor, sensitive mare was in no state to chase down an outlaw. Jacob needed a reliable animal, familiar with the area and less easily agitated.

"Well, gentlemen," Jacob said as he pushed back his chair and stood. "Mr. Colfax and I are going to find Flora Kimball. You can stay put in Elk Springs, going about your regular business, telling yourself the Kimballs don't deserve your help. Or you can set aside your prejudice and join us in rescuing a helpless girl before something worse happens to her."

Jacob wasn't one for making speeches, and he felt self-conscious the entire time those six sets of eyes were on him. But it needed to be said. These men were being selfish and hardhearted, and that poor girl must be scared out of her mind.

He could help her. They could save her. But they needed to get moving.

Joel stood up next to him, also searching the faces of the other men for some sign that Jacob's words had gotten through to them.

Most of them shook their heads or continued eating with their eyes down, not looking at Jacob. But Jacob caught two of the men whispering to each other at the far end of the table. He couldn't hear what was being said, but neither man seemed defiant.

"We'll be off now," Jacob said. "If you change your mind, we'll still take your help at any time. Come on, Joel."

"Wait. We're coming with you."

Jacob was already at the doorway of the Elk Springs Tavern when he heard himself being called back. He turned to see the two men who had been whispering moments before stand up, throw cash down on the table, and move to join him.

"Wait for us," the shorter one said.

The other men watched them go. Jacob felt another stab of disappointment in their behavior. A man should be generous and brave. Even if he thought a neighbor was strange, that shouldn't stop him from keeping the neighbor's daughter safe. But, Jacob reflected, it takes all kinds to make this world, and if some men weren't unscrupulous then he would eventually find himself out of work.

Jacob nodded and gestured for the two men to join them outside.

Standing on the boardwalk lining the dusty street, the shorter one of the two men shook Jacob's hand. "Hey. Name's Zeke. Ezekiel Boyer. And this is my brother-in-law, Boyd Brannigan."

"What can I do for you, gentlemen? I think I made it clear that this young man and I have things to do."

"Right. You did. And we'd like to help. We know Kimball a fair amount and we don't believe what the reverend is claiming."

"And, besides," Boyd put in, "even if it was true, that girl still needs help."

"So we want to go with you. Just tell us what to do."

Jacob looked at Joel, who shrugged. The bounty hunter preferred to work alone, but it looked now as though he'd somehow formed himself a posse. He'd been sincere when entreating the other men to help. If Joel and Zeke and Boyd did actually follow his directions, maybe he could get use out of them.

"All right. Thank you for doing what's right. But from here on, you do exactly as I say at all times. No questions, no protests. Got it?"

They both nodded.

"Let's start with any information you have that might not have been mentioned in there." Jacob gestured with a tip of his chin. "Any thoughts about where to start?"

Boyd spoke up. "I keep coming back to what Sheriff said. He pointed out that it was Kimball's daughter who was kidnapped, not anyone else's. Why is that? Why is Flora special?"

"That's right, isn't there another girl?" Zeke asked. "I think I heard there are two older daughters. Why this one and not the other?"

"Edith," Joel said, nodding. "She's fifteen, I think."

"Could have just been a matter of access. Maybe Flora was just isolated at the exact right time for him to strike," Jacob said. "But you're right. I think that's a good place to start. We're going to have to find the start of the trail to go after him, and maybe we can get some answers once we're there.

"Joel, you know Mr. Kimball the best. Do you think he'd put us up for the night?"

The boy nodded eagerly. "He would. But we should get moving. It's almost an hour's ride out to their place."

Jacob let Joel lead the string of riders out the several miles to Kimball's farm. This stretch of forest looked much the same as the trail and forest they passed through to get to Elk Springs. Jacob spent a very tense hour waiting for some small sound to spook Franny and send them galloping away in the wrong direction. The men stayed quiet on the ride out to the farm, each lost in his own thoughts about the following day, which would be spent chasing the trail of an outlaw.

"Hello, the house!" Joel called as they approached. "Mr. Kimball?"

The front door of the home swung open, revealing a silhouetted figure in the doorway. The figure appeared to be a hulking man, bareheaded but holding a shotgun ready. It occurred to Jacob that if this was Mr. Kimball, Pickens must have been out of his mind to risk kidnapping his daughter.

"Who's there?"

"It's me, Mr. Kimball," Joel said, raising his hand to wave. "Joel Colfax. We heard about Flora and I brought some help."

"Joel? Boy, I haven't seen you in months. Come in."

As soon as he stepped back out of the

doorway the light spilled across his face; Jacob saw the gentle, careworn face of a worried father instead of the menacing patriarch that had been there a moment before.

The four horses were ground-tied in front of the porch, and the men stepped cautiously into the house. Disturbing a family's grief was a difficult thing. They were there to help, to offer hope, but at the same time they didn't want to dismiss or diminish the pain that the members of the family might be feeling.

"Ah, Mr. Brannigan. Mr. Boyer," Kimball said as they entered. "It is good of you to assist. I know what Reverend Fowler has been saying about my family, and I know it must be difficult for you to go against the community.

"But who's your friend?" he asked, looking piercingly at Jacob. "I don't believe you're from Elk Springs."

"No, sir." Jacob doffed his hat and offered his hand. "Name's Jacob Payne."

"He's a bounty hunter," Joel said. "He was passing through Cork when we heard about Flora and agreed to come with me."

Jacob smiled at this slight revision of history, but he let the boy have his claim. Truth be told, Joel likely would have come with or without Jacob anyway.

"Who is it, Father?" a small, sweet voice called from the doorway.

"Come in here, Mary. Come say hello to Joel Colfax and his friends. They're here about Flora."

A petite woman, not much older than Jacob, entered the room from the hallway. She gripped her skirt, as though to anchor herself in the space.

"Gentlemen, may I introduce my wife?"

"Oh," she gasped, clasping her hands to her chest. "Are you really here for Flora? Can you find her?"

Jacob nodded. "I think we can, ma'am. But we have some questions, and we were hoping it wouldn't be too much of an imposition . . ."

"We'll help any way we can. I'm not sure we know anything, though." Mary sat primly on the edge of the rigid chair.

"You might be surprised about what kind of details will help." Jacob pulled his chair closer to where the woman sat. "Take me back to when Pickens showed up here."

She looked at her husband, and he gestured for her to go ahead.

"Mr. Payne, you mustn't think me weak or foolish. We don't know the face of every man that lives in Elk Springs. It didn't occur to me until he had already been here a while that Mr. Pickens might be a stranger."

"I don't think you're foolish at all. I imagine he made himself mighty handy and ingratiating when he got here, didn't he?"

She nodded. "He did."

"How did it happen?"

"Well . . ." She fidgeted, smoothing the fabric of her skirt more than needed. "My husband was out past the pasture, breaking down a tree stump. Mr. Pickens had promised to help, but had found many reasons to stay around the house. He'd busy himself with all sorts of tasks and never make it out to where he was actually needed. It wasn't until after I sent Flora out to the chicken coop that I realized Mr. Pickens was gone, too."

Her husband moved to behind her chair and rested his hand on her shoulder. She reached up to lightly touch his fingers, acknowledging the comfort. It did Jacob's heart good to see such tenderness between the two. For another couple, there might be anger or blame, but the Kimballs seemed united in their pain.

"And when you sent Flora out to get the eggs, that's when he took her?"

Mrs. Kimball nodded. She looked ready to cry, to Jacob's eyes, but held herself together. "I didn't hear any of it," she said in a whisper. "My husband was even farther away. Thank goodness Edith was out near the well at the time and heard the screaming."

Jacob looked around the room, but noticed the other teenage girl was nowhere in sight. "And is Edith okay? Was she attacked as well?"

"No, no. The poor dear is just in shock. She's been in bed since it happened. We've told her it's not her fault and she couldn't have stopped him. But she feels responsible."

"That's ridiculous," Joel said indignantly. "I'll talk to her."

"Not now," Jacob said under his breath. "Let's wait till we find her sister."

"Edith even followed them for a spell, but couldn't keep up. Thank the Lord above. I can't bear to think about losing them both."

"So, then, Edith knows where they went?" Jacob looked hopefully at Mr. Kimball.

He nodded. "She says Pickens was dragging her down the trail that continues up the mountain behind my place." He added to Joel, "The one you all used to explore back in the day."

The young man's eyes grew wide and he stood up excitedly. "Our trail? I know where that is! I can find her."

Jacob, too, felt the first glimmer of hope in

the whole affair. "We'll find her, Mr. Kimball. I promise."

He believed his own words to be true . . . but he hoped they would also find her alive and unharmed.

CHAPTER SEVEN

Jacob woke before dawn, rolling over in the hay and staring up at the roof of the barn. The deep navy-blue night sky was just beginning to grow lighter through the gaps in the walls. The Kimballs' rooster out in the chicken coop was beginning his morning ritual. The four men would need to be on the trail as soon as possible. Since they had already missed the prime window immediately after the kidnapping, it'd be best to do this as prudently and carefully as possible.

As he rolled over and got to his knees, Jacob thought he heard the gentle thuds of horse hooves approaching the barn. Immediately he wrapped his fingers around the handle of his revolver. Who would be riding up to this out-of-the-way farm so early in the morning unless they meant to catch the family unawares?

"What—?" Joel said as he woke.

"Shh," Jacob warned, gesturing for the boy to stay down as he crept to the wall of the barn. There, right about the height of his eyes, was a small gap in the boards. The bounty hunter held his gun ready and watched for the approaching stranger.

Within seconds, both Boyd and Zeke were armed and at his side, waiting for whatever Jacob instructed them to do.

The horse and rider got closer. Through the narrow crack, Jacob watched a stranger dressed all in black approach the house, slowing as he got closer, eyes darting in every direction looking for something. He didn't announce himself. He didn't make a sound as he dismounted. He drew his gun and crept toward the house slowly.

Jacob didn't like it one bit.

Just as he was about to confront the stranger, next to him Zeke said, bewilderedly, "That's Reverend Fowler."

"You're sure?"

He nodded.

"Go greet him," Jacob instructed. "He needs to know he's not alone."

He waited in the dark barn, watching carefully as Zeke rounded the corner, exited through the wide door, and called to the new arrival.

"Reverend Fowler! What are you doing here?"

The man in black started, surprised to be seen at all, let alone spoken to. "What? I—"

"You wouldn't be here looking to join our posse, would you?"

"Of course not." The reverend seemed offended at the suggestion.

Jacob stepped out through to doorway, revolver in hand, eyes boring into the newcomer. "Then what is it we can help you with?"

"I . . . well, I . . ." he spluttered. The reverend closed his mouth, stood up straighter, and adjusted his coat. "I've come to offer my condolences to Mr. Kimball for his loss and extend to him the path to the kingdom of heaven before it's too late."

Jacob held back a bark of laughter. "Fine," he said. "Let's go see what Mr. Kimball has to say about that."

"No, I—"

"Oh, we're going with you, Mister—Fowler, is it? We need to speak to the man before we leave to rescue his daughter. I'm sure he won't mind having us both there."

Jacob grabbed the upper arm of Reverend Fowler none too gently and marched him toward the front door of the farmhouse, with the rest of his party following closely behind.

As they climbed the steps to the porch, the front door opened and Mrs. Kimball stepped out with an armful of cookware.

"Let me help you with that, ma'am," Joel said as he moved to relieve her of her burden. From her hands he took a heavy pitcher of steaming water and a wide ceramic basin.

"Oh, thank you, Joel. Let me go get you boys some towels and soap now."

Jacob, his fingers still gripping the reverend's arm, watched as Joel set up the basin on the rail of the porch.

The kid grinned at him as he realized what Mrs. Kimball had brought them. "We have time to wash up before we go, right, Mr. Payne?"

"Yeah, go ahead." It might be the last chance they get at real soap and hot water for a while; they might as well take the extra five minutes to enjoy it.

Mrs. Kimball returned to the porch, carrying further supplies for her guests, with her husband right behind her. Joel busied himself with the water while Jacob handled the visitor.

"My wife tells me—" Mr. Kimball began, stopping when he noticed Reverend Fowler. "What can I do for you, Reverend?" he asked, his voice cold.

Reverend Fowler shook off Jacob's grip and again straightened his jacket. With his arm now free, he removed his hat, nodding politely to Mrs. Kimball before dropping his voice in reverence. "Mr. Kimball, I've come to pray with you. To offer myself as an intercessor with our Lord Jesus Christ, on behalf of your family and your dearly departed Flora."

Mr. Kimball frowned. "Now, my Flora might be dear to me, and she might have temporarily departed this farm, but I don't like your tone. I don't like what you are insinuating."

"I understand it may be difficult to accept," Reverend Fowler said, placing his hand over his heart. "But this is a chance, sir. An opportunity. God has spared your life and granted you more time on earth to accept him as your Lord and Savior and—"

"Hold on now just a minute." Kimball clenched one of his giant, meaty hands into a fist. "My God is the same as your God. You can't come here, come onto *my* land, and tell me I am any less saved than you." He punctuated his sentence by stepping forward, pointing his finger at the reverend and pushing it hard into his chest.

Reverend Fowler stumbled backward a couple steps. Jacob watched, ready to break them apart if necessary. Though Kimball may be in the right, angering and attacking the town preacher was not a step that would serve him.

"Reverend Fowler," Jacob said. "I think maybe this is not the place for you. Why don't you go on back to town and pray from there?"

Kimball glared at his visitor, but kept his lips pursed, guarding himself against saying anything he might regret.

"Wait, wait, wait!" the reverend said, raising his hands above his head. "Wait. If you won't let me pray with you, at least listen to what I have to say."

"Not if it is insulting this good man in his own home," Jacob said.

"No," Reverend Fowler answered, "not that. Though I despair of you recovering the poor girl unharmed and intact, if you are insistent on trying, you should listen to what I have to say."

Jacob exchanged a glance with Kimball. "Why should we listen to you?" he said.

"Believe me." Reverend Fowler placed a

hand over his heart again, all but pleading with Jacob. "I have no wish to harm you men, or to let you walk into a situation unprepared. I have had several conversations with this lecherous character Pickens and I believe my knowledge could help you."

"Mr. Payne, the water is getting cold," Joel called from the end of the porch where he had been getting cleaned up. "You want to come use what's left?"

"Oh heavens," Mrs. Kimball said, bustling over. "Let me warm some more up for you."

"I'd like some of that," Boyd said, crossing to the rail. "If it's not too much trouble, ma'am."

As this small interruption occurred, Jacob took the opportunity to observe Reverend Fowler closer. When he thought no one was looking, when his own attention was trained on the boy and the soapy water, the reverend's expression softened. His shoulders had dropped and his eyes took on a hopeful gleam. In that small moment of unguardedness, Jacob saw what he believed to be the true motivation behind the man's visit.

Reverend Fowler may be pompous and condescending, but he was still a man of God who wanted to help, misguided though he may be.

"All right, Reverend," Jacob said. "Why don't you and me take a seat over here on the steps and you can fill me in on what you learned from Pickens?"

He gestured to the steps at their feet. Reverend Fowler blanched briefly, then bent down to haphazardly dust off the step with his hat and gingerly sat. Jacob stood on the dirt at his feet, put one foot up on the step, and leaned forward on his knee. Zeke leaned on the rail, casually eavesdropping but offering no input. Kimball sat on the other side of the reverend, gun still in hand but staying quiet.

"When did you first meet Pickens?" Jacob began.

Reverend Fowler glanced askance at the muzzle of the gun pointed in his direction. While Jacob himself would never point a gun idly at a neighbor, he noticed that Kimball's hands were nowhere near the trigger and suspected the older man was simply trying to scare the other.

"Well, he, um . . ." Reverend Fowler shot one last glance at Kimball before clearing his throat and directing his answer to Jacob. "Pickens stopped by the rectory not long after he showed up in Elk Springs. The very day he arrived, I think. You may not believe it, but he would not stop talking about that rumored Herron gold mine."

"You don't say?" Zeke answered, rolling his eyes a little.

"It's true," the reverend continued. "He was asking everyone in town if they had heard about the mine. And I believe at least one man pointed the way to this very farm."

"Yes, Reverend," Jacob said with a sigh. "We know all that. Other men in town have already given us those details."

"Did these other men tell you what was in the telegram he sent to Santa Fe?"

Jacob and Kimball exchanged a glance.

"Might as well get to it, Reverend. What do you know?"

He looked at the faces all expectantly watching him and blanched, as though he only just realized the situation he had put himself in.

"Well, as I'm sure is no surprise," Reverend Fowler said pompously, regaining some of his color, "the man is illiterate. He demanded I write down what he wanted the telegram to say, and I have to admit I succumbed to his threats."

"It's fine, Reverend," Jacob said, growing

impatient. "We understand why you did it. But what did it *say*?"

"Well, it seems this Pickens character must have accomplices of some sort. He asked his recipient to meet him on this very mountain."

"That means we may be walking into a gang," Boyd said. "What'll we do?"

"Act fast," Jacob said. "We might be able to get to Flora before whoever this accomplice is even arrives. That's plenty to be getting on with. I think it's time we hit the trail."

"Wait, um, Mr. Payne." Joel rushed to his side. "You think maybe we should ask about a horse?"

"A horse?" Mr. Kimball asked, overhearing. "Don't you have a horse?"

"I do, sir." Jacob hesitated. He hated admitting any weakness, even if it was just in his choice of horse. "She is a bit skittish, though. She's borrowed from a friend and I'm not sure—"

"Say no more. I have just the thing."

Jacob followed his host, once again grateful for kind strangers.

CHAPTER EIGHT

Joel led the group of armed men silently down the trail, taking them deeper into the mountains. They had been trekking through the woods for nearly an hour now, with no sign of slowing. The trail was narrow, so small that Jacob was surprised Joel didn't have more trouble following it. He must have spent innumerable hours of his youth exploring this side of the mountain with Flora.

Jacob brought up the rear of their posse, trailing behind Zeke by about twenty feet as he grew accustomed to his new mount. Kimball had been generous enough to loan the bounty hunter one of his stallions. Franny was boarded comfortably in the Kimballs' barn, waiting for Jacob to return. When he had rode off that morning she seemed perfectly happy to be left alone, safe and unmolested.

Instead of a fragile, skittish mare, Jacob's new mount was both mellow and eager to get going. The gorgeous creature's name was Blaze, and though Jacob had only just met him, he was completely at peace with trusting the horse. Indeed, the two seemed to already be experiencing a unique bond. Just the smallest of pressure from Jacob's knees or heels and Blaze obeyed immediately. The horse was at home on the trail and under his new rider.

Jacob was still a little on edge, still worried a tree branch might fall close by and spook his new ride, but told himself he could handle it. Hopefully the stallion was more used to this forest and its sounds than Franny had been, but even if not, he already trusted this horse more. Regardless, Jacob would put up with any obstacles if it meant he was able to get to Flora soon enough.

Up ahead, Jacob heard Joel let out a long, low whistle.

"Mr. Payne?" he called.

Jacob flicked the reins and trotted up along the side of the trail to stand next to Joel. "What did you find?"

Joel had dismounted and was walking slowly

a few feet farther along the trail. He didn't even need to answer before Jacob saw what caused him to stop their trek. Ten feet ahead, the dirt trail narrowed even further and passed between rocks. A couple sizable boulders and at least a dozen large stones waited in piles on either side.

Splattered on the rocks, in at least three different places that Jacob could identify from where his horse stood, dark dried blood told the grisly tale of the previous passersby. It wasn't a lot of blood, but it was enough. Whoever spilled this could have a very serious injury and needed their help. If they were still alive.

Joel sniffed. Jacob looked at him sharply, but the young man wasn't facing him. He may be deliberately hiding his tears, but Jacob could guess.

"Let's just remember," Jacob said, "we have no way of knowing if this blood is Flora's. It could be anyone's. It could be an animal's, for all we know. For that matter, we don't even know if it was left recently. Once it's dry, all blood looks the same until it rains."

"I suppose that's true," Joel muttered.

"It rained last week," Boyd offered from behind.

Jacob glared at him. That wasn't helping calm Joel.

"The smartest thing to do," Jacob continued, "is to follow along this trail toward the Herron mine. Same as we were planning. We're like to find more clues along the way, if your guess as to where they're going is right, Joel."

"I never did catch why we're going this way," Zeke said.

"We're going to where the Herron mine is supposed to be."

"Yeah, but . . . it doesn't exist, does it? I heard that dozens of men combed these mountains looking for it and never found a lick of gold."

"No, you're right," Joel said. "It doesn't exist." He rummaged in his saddlebag for a canteen and took a long swig of water before continuing. "I don't know where the initial story came from, but lots of men, and later entire families, came out this way looking for gold. That's how Elk Springs came to be in the first place. A settlement for the gold mine—if there had even been a mine. It's named after the fella that claimed there was a mine here in the first place, sending all those fools out searching in the wilderness. Matthew Herron."

"So then . . ." Boyd removed his hat and scratched his head. "Where are we going?"

"Like I said, I've known the Kimball family

since I was about five years old. My father spent a few years looking for the mine and we lived here on the mountain. Flora and me used to play all over their farm, and as we got older we were allowed to venture farther and farther away.

"We had heard all the stories, of course. Growing up in Elk Springs it was like a myth in the back of your mind at all times. 'Look for the Herron mine.' Everyone knew by then that it didn't exist, but they had been in the habit for so long it lingered.

"So, when Flora and I were ten or eleven, we were allowed to venture past the Kimball property line. We spent a lot of time in this forest and on this very trail. We found a cave—it's only a little bit farther up. It's just a cave. It doesn't even go that deep into the mountain, but we started pretending it was the Herron mine. It started out as a joke, but that's what we called it between the two of us.

"Maybe someone else heard us. I know Mr. Kimball called the cave the same thing, but he knew it was just our play spot. Somehow word that Flora knew where the Herron mine is must have gotten out into Elk Springs."

"So that's why we're heading down this trail," Jacob concluded.

"That's right." Joel nodded. "And I hope I'm not wrong. If she's not at this cave, I don't have any other idea where he could have taken her."

"Don't worry, Joel. We'll find her." Jacob believed his own words. "I don't want to assume this is her blood spilled on the mountain, but if nothing else it's a good indication that people came this way."

"I don't understand why she would agree to help him in the first place," Joel said, disappointment and confusion clear on his face. "The Flora I used to know was independent and strong."

"You have to remember, though, that she always felt safe with you, right? If she knows that you're not going to beat her for expressing an opinion, she will be more likely to be herself. But Pickens probably started with violence. She's only seventeen. Does she know how to use a gun?"

Joel shook his head.

"There. You see?" Jacob said. "Going along with the outlaw is just her way of protecting herself. There's not much else she could do if she wanted to stay alive."

"I guess that's so." Joel looked thoughtfully down the trail, farther into the forest where they were headed. "Maybe this blood is a sign she's finally starting to fight back."

"Maybe so," Jacob agreed. "From everything you and your father have said, she seems like a gutsy girl. Let's not worry too much."

Joel nodded. "You're right. Let's keep going."

He mounted his horse again and took the lead, walking slowly down the trail, looking right and left for another clue that Flora and Pickens had passed by this spot. The group stayed quiet. Around them, birds twittered to each other. Every so often one of the horses would huff a deep breath or a small woodland animal would disturb the brush just out of their sight.

If it weren't for the stress of being yet again on the trail of an outlaw, Jacob might have actually enjoyed this ride. The forests of the White Mountains were beautiful. The trail curved up and around to the right, the men climbing farther up the mountain. The air was thinner here than Jacob was used to. Just before the trail curved around again to the left, Joel let out a strangled cry.

He quickly jumped off his horse and tore up the trail.

"What is it?" Jacob asked in a carrying whisper. Since he wasn't sure what Joel had spotted, he didn't know how close the enemy might be. "Joel!"

The young man darted ahead to something just off the side of the trail. He crouched down, hesitated, and then snatched something off the ground. A small scrap of something colorful that Jacob couldn't make out at this distance.

When Joel turned back toward the rest of the group, his face displayed pure fury. His cheeks were flushed, and even from this distance Jacob could see that he was clenching his jaw. The muscles in the boy's neck stood out as he stomped back toward the others.

He held out his hands in front of him, the slip of color now draped across his palms. It was a narrow lavender ribbon, maybe eighteen inches long. As he drew closer, Jacob noticed that one of the ends was frayed and he wondered where the rest of the ribbon had gone.

"It's Flora's," Joel said as he approached. "It's Flora's. I remember when she got this hair ribbon for her birthday. She loved this color. How could she have lost it?"

"Maybe she didn't lose it," Jacob suggested. "Maybe she deliberately dropped it."

In a moment, Joel's entire expression changed from despair to hope. He clenched the ribbon in his fist and smiled at Jacob. "You're right. And maybe this end is frayed because she tried dropping some pieces earlier on the trail and we just missed them."

Jacob nodded encouragingly. "That would be real smart of her."

Joel's eyes shone. "Flora is a smart girl."

Jacob smiled. "So, now we know for sure we're on the right trail."

"Yes!"

"Let's not keep her waiting."

Joel moved quickly, jumping back on his horse and taking the lead again as they continued on the trail toward the cave he and Flora had called the Herron Mine.

They rode more quickly now that they were sure they were on the correct path. The horses carried them up and up the rocky trail, winding around curves of the mountain and between the trees. The sun climbed in the sky and Jacob wondered if they should stop to eat.

Joel held up a hand, pausing their advance.

CHAPTER NINE

When Joel paused their advance, Jacob dismounted, tossed the reins to Zeke, and crept up on foot to the young man at the head of their posse.

"What is it?" he whispered, scanning the area.

Joel pointed. "The cave is just past there. Look!"

Jacob followed where the young man indicated. Farther up, the trail continued into the dark, dense forest. For a brief moment he didn't see anything unusual. At a glance, there was no clear reason why Joel had stopped at this spot. The light peeking in through the forest canopy ahead flickered and flashed, making Jacob think he saw movement where there wasn't any.

He sniffed the air, but couldn't make out anything out of the ordinary. Earth, forest, and animal scents all wove around them, but other than Joel on his horse next to him, Jacob didn't smell anything that alluded to Pickens or anyone else being nearby.

But his gut said differently. The bounty hunter kept his gaze trained down the length of the trail to where Joel had pointed as he crept forward a little farther on foot, darting behind the trunk of a large tree in case whatever Joel had seen was watching back. The longer he looked the more he noticed.

Just through the trees, Jacob noticed the trail about thirty feet ahead curving around an enormous boulder. From this distance he was guessing, but the boulder likely would tower several feet above his own head. It seemed to form a virtual wall of rock presumably continuing past the curve and along the trail farther up the mountain. Small cracks in the boulder revealed the smallest weeds and tiny plants trying to take hold, but the stone seemed nearly impenetrable.

It would be the perfect cover and protection for an outlaw.

Just as he was about to turn back to Joel to ask what he had noticed, movement caught his eye. The flash of a purple skirt wafted into view from behind the boulder before winking out of sight again. There was someone there. Jacob had no doubt he had seen a skirt. There was a woman just out of sight.

He prayed it was Flora Kimball.

Jacob strained his ears to listen. He almost thought he could identify a faint mumble of conversation, but couldn't hear anything more above the horses' heavy breathing and occasional pawing at the ground.

He had to get closer. But he couldn't leave the others behind.

He crept back to Joel and whispered quick instructions, then repeated the same to Boyd and Zeke. He needed the men to drop anything holding them back so they could be the most nimble on their approach to rescue the girl. The men would find a tree and cover, far off the trail, to leave their horses. Then they could all move forward quietly to inspect what was on the other side of that boulder and hiding farther up the mountain.

Once those steps were underway, Jacob was on his own again. He moved off the path and through the trees, winding his way downhill. His revolver in hand, the bounty hunter kept a focused watch on his prey—or where he hoped he'd find his prey—while he moved to a better position. He took a wide, arching path so he could observe while staying out of sight, downwind, and flank the mysterious camp. As he progressed downhill, winding between the trees, more and more of the scene on the trail became clear. From this angle, it was evident that the boulder had been hiding quite a lot. Joel's eye had been sharp, far sharper than the bounty hunter's.

Jacob spied the remains of a campfire, a pile of saddlebags and two horses tied not far away. But in spite of this evidence of habitation on the trail, he could not actually see any humans. He would have almost thought that he had imagined the purple dress, the site was so quiet. But no. He was sure he had seen it. There must be someone nearby.

Where had she gone?

The boulder itself curved into the side of the mountain, creating a rocky wall that the trail wound around. The rock wall disappeared into a narrow crevice that marked the opening of the cave. It was wider than a man, but not by much. Just a small break in the rock that continued down the length of the trail, forming a wall and cliff on the mountain face.

Joel, Boyd, and Zeke reached him in his

hiding spot just downhill from the empty campsite.

"I'm sure I saw movement," Joel insisted in a whisper.

"I did, too," Jacob answered. "They must have gone back in the cave."

"But that was Flora, right? You saw the dress, right? It matched her hair ribbon that I found."

Jacob nodded, keeping his eyes trained on the split in the rock where the cave hid who-knew-what.

If he had been on his own, Jacob might have rushed the group or gone in guns blazing and put himself at risk. Or perhaps he wouldn't have seen the hiding place at all. With Joel, and the other men, he was not only better informed, but also safer. He was warned about the cave, and he had the security of three other gunmen to help him cover the area.

"How deep is that cave, Joel? How many men do you think he could be hiding?"

"Oh, it's big enough for quite a group, but there's only the two horses."

"That's true, but—"

Jacob's planning was interrupted by the sound of yelling coming from up near the camp-site. He shut his mouth quickly and ducked down as three figures came stumbling out from the mouth of the cave and into the open campsite.

A blond girl, her hair hanging loosely around her shoulders, her purple calico dress dusty and torn in places, stalked out from the dark crevice, walking backward toward the campsite. Her right hand was held high above her head, and though Jacob couldn't see for sure from this distance, she appeared to be wielding a weapon of some kind. Maybe a rock. On its own, held in her small hand, the rock might not do that much damage, but Jacob had seen how much power and strength a woman could have when she was in danger. He would bet on the girl in this situation any day. After all, she had already figured out how to free herself from whatever binding they'd most likely had her in.

Two men, dirty and rough, stalked out of the cave after her, moving to either side. She was trying to walk backward, away from her pursuers, and kept checking over her shoulder for where she was going to step next. Jacob found himself holding his breath, anxious for her to gain the upper hand. Should he move to help? The two men both had guns trained on her, and a sudden movement from him might cause one of them to pull the trigger.

Flora continued her backward stagger. Trying to look in three different directions would prove difficult for anyone, and, sure enough, she put her foot down in the wrong place, stumbled, and fell into the dirt. The outlaws—one must be Pickens—stalked toward her. Their lecherous grins made Jacob shudder.

"Flora!" Joel cried in a strangled whisper.

Jacob put his hand on the boy's shoulder to keep him from rushing out and revealing their hiding places.

"We'll get her, Joel. But we have to be smart and plan it."

"Now! We have to get her now!"

Jacob nodded, not bothering to try to calm the boy down. If all went according to plan, in just a few moments he could have the girl. It was time to take their shot.

"Stay where you are, son. It won't do Flora any good to have you shot because those despicable men spotted you."

"But—"

"This is our best chance," Jacob said, speaking to Boyd and Zeke. "Joel and I take the one on the left. You two men take the one on the right. If we all shoot at the same time, they won't have a chance to fight back, even if one of us misses."

Jacob had to admit it wasn't the best of plans, but it would do in a pinch.

"Watch out for Flora," Joel said.

"She should be out of the way. She'll be fine. Don't shoot to kill, though. If possible, we need to let the law determine these men's fate. Everyone understand?"

The faces around him all nodded with the same look of grim determination.

"Ready? On my count," Jacob whispered, taking careful aim. "One. Two . . ."

Before he could finish his count, they were interrupted by the sound of hooves galloping toward the camp. Jacob's stomach dropped.

CHAPTER TEN

"Hold your fire," Jacob said to his men.

He lowered his own revolver and darted ahead a few steps to the next wide tree trunk between Flora, the men who held her captive, and himself.

"Damn," he muttered.

They had missed their chance at easily overpowering the villains while there were only two of them. The horses he had heard approaching came around the curve in the trail from the opposite direction—three more dirty, rugged men, riding into camp from the opposite side of the mountain. Jacob could see at a glance that these were not men from Elk Springs. These newcomers had spent the night outside, undoubtedly after having ridden the several hundred miles from Santa Fe. Jacob was glad he wasn't any closer, if not just because he wouldn't want to have to smell those fellas.

But now Jacob and his team were outnumbered. Five to four—not even including the encumbrance of helping Flora get away on top of overpowering her captors. The easy moment had passed him by and now he would have to come up with a better plan.

He needed to get closer. If he could get close enough, Jacob would be able to listen to their plan. The more information he had the easier it would be for him to identify their weaknesses and infiltrate or ambush them.

Jacob looked around. The forest wasn't dense enough for him to be able to get much closer. The trees in the White Mountains were primarily some variation of pine. They were tall and straight, with increasingly smaller branches as they stretched toward the sky. He could dart from tree to tree, but in the spaces between— or even his broad shoulders sticking out around the width of the skinny trunks—he could be found out. He could send Joel, who was thinner and possibly quicker, but he wasn't sure the boy would remember all the details to report back.

He didn't have any other options. Every hesitation put Flora more at risk.

Jacob glanced once more at the five outlaws now congregating around the mouth of the cave. Not one of them even glanced in his direction, so sure were they that they had gotten away with their kidnapping. And for good reason, Jacob thought to himself crossly, though maybe he could use that to his advantage now. He, Joel, and the other two men hadn't even started on the trail for almost two days after Flora had been taken. That would have been plenty long enough to lull Pickens into a feeling of security. Given time, his men to reinforce him, and this cave, of course Pickens was feeling invincible. Of course he wasn't concerned about any rustling noises in the forest around him.

The man's arrogance and obliviousness would be just what led to his demise, Jacob vowed to himself.

He looked back at the other three men and caught Boyd's eye. He held up his hand, indicating that they should wait where they were, then pointed to himself, and farther up the incline. Boyd nodded, his hand on his gun, glancing anxiously between Jacob and the group of ruffians past him.

Jacob was satisfied. The men would remain where they were, but keep an eye on him as he went, providing him cover in case things went wrong.

And he couldn't afford a single thing to go wrong. Not anymore. He had already missed too many chances to rescue the poor girl.

The bounty hunter all but tiptoed through the ground cover and dried pine needles that blanketed the mountain beneath his feet. Three long steps to the next-closest tree trunk large enough to shelter him—most of him, anyway. Once there, he paused to listen for any indication he had been spotted.

Nothing.

A peek around the trunk to check his progress and then four more loping steps to the next wide trunk. The trees were thinning and he had to stand sideways, his right shoulder leaning against the wood, to ensure he stayed hidden. Jacob took off his hat and held it against his chest, worried that the brim might have stuck out and given him away.

He slowed his breath and listened.

"Manage to beat it out of her yet?" one of the men asked.

Jacob heard a shuffle—leather, maybe some metal—and hooves pawing at the ground. He couldn't risk poking his head around the tree this close. The group of outlaws was now only about thirty feet up the slope from him. Judging by the sounds, though, Jacob would guess that the men were busying themselves in making camp. Most likely planning to stick around this spot for awhile.

"No," a second voice answered.

There was a muted *thud* and a tiny whimper that made Jacob think that Flora had been kicked or punched. His temper flared and it took all his patience to keep himself from rushing up the hill, guns blazing. He calmed himself—getting Flora killed in a fire fight wouldn't help anyone.

"She still claims it's not actually a mine," the second voice continued. "I dunno, Morris. Maybe she's telling the truth."

"Maybe. But then, if she is that means we have no more use for her."

Jacob could practically hear the sneer in the man's voice.

"Just let me go," a sweet, feminine voice sobbed. "Let me go home. I showed you where the mine was supposed to be."

"*Supposed* to be," the second voice repeated. By now Jacob guessed that was likely his man, full name Homer Pickens. "But I don't yet see even a flake of gold in my hand, missy. Do you?"

"I don't know how to mine gold!" she

cried. Jacob was gratified to hear some strength and sass come into her voice. The girl had a backbone yet. "I'm just a girl. You think if I knew how to mine gold I'd just leave it in there?"

"She has a point, Homer." A mumbling third man joined the conversation.

Jacob snickered quietly to himself, imagining the scene. The girl had some spunk, he had to give her that.

"Shut up!"

A piercing yelp split the air as Jacob heard the unmistakable sound of a hand slapping flesh.

"My lip!" she cried. "I'm bleeding!"

Jacob felt another wave of fury, this one dwarfing the last, rolling over him. Robbing banks or rustling cattle was one thing. Though he didn't agree with it, Jacob understood what might drive a man to that kind of activity. But laying a hand on a woman? Assaulting a delicate creature? Not to mention doing all this to her while she's tied up and unable to even run away from such violence.

No, these men would pay. There was no excusing that behavior.

This would take some strategy, he reminded himself. He and his small posse would need thoughtful planning to take them by surprise or to sneak in to rescue the girl.

Jacob retreated back to where the others were waiting. He shook his head in answer to Joel's questioning look.

"We can't stay here," he said. "We—"

"I'm not leaving her!" Joel hissed. "You go back, if you must. I'm going to find a way to rescue Flora."

"Joel, I'm not going back to Elk Springs. Keep your voice down. We just can't stay in this spot. It's too exposed. Let's go back to the horses and reassess."

Joel looked like he wanted to protest. He kept glancing back to where Flora had disappeared down the dark mouth of the cave and wasn't moving his feet. Jacob firmly wrapped his fingers around the boy's upper arm and dragged him away.

CHAPTER ELEVEN

Jacob dragged the boy away from the mouth of the cave and led the group around the curve of the mountain, between the trees, traveling as quietly as they could to not draw attention to themselves. Jacob had a feeling that the men would be distracted for quite a while—what with looking for gold, fighting among themselves, and keeping Flora in line—but it still behooved him to be cautious.

When they had reached the trail again, now on the other side of the boulder, Boyd took the lead back to where their four horses had been tied.

"We've got to go back," Joel insisted with a hiss.

Jacob unbuckled the leather cover of the pack on Blaze and pulled out a side of jerky. He tossed a piece to Joel and took a bite himself, chewing slowly while he thought out the next steps.

"We will go back, son," he said patiently. "But you saw those men. Five of them. With cave cover, to boot. Now that we know more of their plan, we can take advantage of it."

"What's their plan?" Zeke asked.

Jacob explained what he had overheard about the mine and how they thought they needed Flora.

"That's ridiculous," Joel said. "There has never been a mine there."

"I know that. You know that. *Flora* knows that, and said as much repeatedly to her thick-headed kidnappers. Seems they don't want to believe it."

"But what are they going to do to Flora while they're trying to find the gold?"

Jacob shook his head. He didn't want to put it into words.

"What will they do when they finally accept that she can't help them?"

Jacob just shook his head again.

Joel grabbed Jacob's arm, pulling on him, starting to panic.

"Here's what I'm thinking," Jacob said, not answering Joel directly. "They look like they'll be going in and out of the cave, since they set up camp outside. Which means that at some point, not all five of them will be together. One or two of them will be isolated if we watch carefully enough. We just need to wait for the right moment, overpower the one or two that remain outside and take it from there."

Boyd nodded. "Yeah. I think that could work."

"But we have to time it exactly," Jacob emphasized. "Too late or too early and we could find all five of those madmen swarming down on us."

"Do you know who they are?" This from Zeke.

Jacob shook his head. "No, I don't, none except Homer Pickens. Which means I'd rather we don't kill them if we don't have to. I always want to take them alive if possible, but more so now while we don't even know their identities. Standing by idly while a girl is held hostage is not admirable, certainly, but it's also not a crime worthy of death."

Joel grumbled under his breath about this last part, but Jacob chose to ignore it. The kid was under a lot of pressure and had likely never been in such high stakes before.

"Let's not have any confusion," he said. "I will decide when the right moment is. You all will follow my cue, my lead, and my instructions. If I detect any mutiny among you"—he pointed to each man in turn—"I will turn my considerable skill to subduing you first. Believe me when I tell you I am more than capable of taking all three of you on if I have to." He said this last directly to Joel.

"Got it, boss," Boyd said, answering for the others.

Jacob kept his gaze on Joel, and the young man finally nodded.

"All right. Follow me."

He led the group of men through the trees, back toward the outlaws' campsite, then back around the other side of it. Jacob cut his own path through the trees to the right and uphill of the boulder, up over where the cave entrance cut into the mountain. The slope of the mountain grew steep as the four made their way back to the cave. The overhang was bare of trees, and even the low shrubs were sparse.

"Leave your hats," Jacob instructed in a whisper.

They left a pile at the foot of one of the pine trees and crawled forward on their bellies. Elbows pulling them forward along the dirt, the men stayed as silent as possible. From behind him, Jacob heard Zeke blow out air through pursed lips, likely pushing a weed or spider web out of his face.

They slowly, carefully approached the edge, knowing that just below them, only ten feet away, were five men who could easily kill them as soon as they saw them. Jacob gestured the men forward, so all four were lying low to the ground in a row, looking over the edge to the campsite.

Now all they had to do was wait for the right moment. Once there was but a single outlaw outside the cave, Jacob would simply jump down the few feet to the ground below and take him prisoner.

It should be easy. It would just take time.

At the moment, four of the five men, plus the girl, were sitting in the dirt around the campsite. One of the men was roasting something over the embers and the others were fiddling with their various weapons or tools. To Jacob's eyes it seemed like they were all just wasting time, waiting for something.

One of the men's voices floated up to them. "I didn't ride all the way out here from Santa Fe for no gold, Pickens. If Jack can't find nothing down there you'll be compensating me by other means."

"Oh shut up, Morris," Pickens answered from across the campsite. "You've traveled farther for far less. That whore of yours in New Orleans ain't worth half what you can get here."

"And yet I still got nothin' in my hand."

"The gold is in there. Four different people told me this here girl knew where the mine is."

"Sure don't look that way to me. Looks like we been lied to. Are you a fool, Pickens, a fool who believes little girls?"

"Let's see what little Flora has to say." Pickens stood up and crossed the space in two steps to leer over her.

"That's Miss Kimball to you," she said, her voice pure venom.

Such courage was rewarded with a hard slap across the face. Jacob winced when he heard the crack, but silently cheered the girl for standing her ground.

"Don't you talk back to me, girl."

There was a beat of silence, Flora's head hung down, recovering from the blow. When she looked back up at Pickens, Jacob could see that something in her had broken. She no longer cared to keep her captors happy or to even ensure her own safety. Brow furrowed, she glared at the outlaw with fury, holding his gaze directly. Without breaking eye contact she lifted both feet up. With her ankles still bound she had less leverage, but she still managed to slam the full strength of her legs into the man's knee.

Jacob thought he heard something go *crack*. Pickens collapsed to the dirt.

Two of the other men hurried forward to subdue the girl, yelling and cursing at her, but Pickens stopped them.

"She's mine," he said darkly, holding his hand up to hold them back.

Flora whimpered as she watched Pickens climb painfully to his feet.

"No," she whispered.

He limped toward her, bearing down, looming over her. Flora scooted backward in the dirt, moving awkwardly with her hands bound behind her back, her feet still bound at the ankles. She moved away in this fashion until her back hit the enormous boulder, knocking her head in the surprise. Pickens reached her easily, grabbing one ankle and pulling her violently toward him. He grabbed the skirt of her dress in both hands and ripped it roughly all the way from her hem to her waist.

"No!" Flora cried, sounding truly terrified for the first time.

CHAPTER TWELVE

No!" Joel cried.

"Shhh. Joel. You have to keep your voice—"

"No, I won't. They can't do that to her. I can't let them!"

"Joel, you've got to—"

Zeke reached up and wrapped his arms around Joel's leg. The kid tried to kick him off, but Zeke managed to hang on, wrestling the kid to the ground and at least temporarily stopping him from giving away their position. But the twenty-year-old was too strong, too wiry. He struggled and pulled and slipped out of the older man's grasp.

Jacob tried again to calm the kid down, but Joel was inconsolable. And he was strong. He easily shook off Jacob's hands as he climbed to his feet.

"She needs me!" he cried, jumping down to the campsite below.

Jacob ducked his head, praying that the other men would think to do the same. They had to hide from view, for when the outlaws would inevitably look up to where the boy had come from.

"Joel Colfax!" Flora cried in amazement.

Jacob put out his hands, stopping Boyd and Zeke from going after Joel. There was no sense in all of them putting themselves in danger. If he was careful there might still be a way to salvage this. If Joel would just . . .

Jacob and the other two men listened helplessly. There was no response from the kid. With his head down and hidden, Jacob could only hear what was happening. He would have to guess. There were several heavy thuds that sounded like punches to his gut or back, along with a *crack!* that certainly marked a hit to the boy's head.

"Joel," cried Flora, subdued.

Jacob shook his head to himself. Even without seeing what was happening, it was clear that whatever men had been outside the cave when the kid jumped down were plenty to trounce him.

"Lord God in Heaven," Boyd said under his breath.

"Dammit!" Jacob scrunched up his face, closing his eyes against the reality of his new situation. With Joel now captured, their entire balance of power was in doubt. "Damn," he whispered again.

He gestured to the other two men to get their attention. When they looked at him, Jacob pointed back down the mountain and began to crawl backward, out of sight and out of hearing of the outlaws below. Satisfied that he heard the other men following him, he continued his climb.

He had to start over with a new plan. Again.

Once he was a sufficient distance away, Jacob got to his feet, dusted the dirt off his front, and strode another dozen feet into the forest for better cover.

Zeke and Boyd were close behind him. Their searching looks reminded Jacob of how little his team was prepared for this kind of stand-off. These two men had likely never dealt with outlaws of Pickens's ilk and were looking to Jacob to show them how it was done.

"Well . . ." Jacob began slowly. He took a

deep breath and let it out as quietly as he could. "This complicates things."

"We can't . . . you're not serious?" Boyd said fearfully.

"What? That it'll be difficult to get Flora *and* Joel back? Why the hell do you think we're even here, Boyd?"

"Just us three against them five? I dunno, Jacob. We had a chance when there was just two of them. We mighta could done something with Joel still with us. But now? I just don't see how we're going to free them kids."

"There must be a way," Jacob insisted. "There's always a way."

"No. Huh-uh." Boyd shook his head. "It's over."

"Yeah, Boyd's right," Zeke said, nodding grimly. "We all got families. We can't be putting ourselves at risk any more than we already have. My wife is expecting me home. You gonna be the one to tell her I got shot trying to rescue some stranger?"

"Let me ask you something, Mr. Boyer. You got a daughter?"

Zeke nodded.

"A son?"

"Three boys and a girl." He stood up a little straighter and puffed up his chest with pride.

Jacob noted the shine in his eyes when he mentioned his kids. This was a man who cherished his family and was proud of them. A man who valued his home life. The kind of man on whom America was built.

"And"—Jacob lowered his voice even more and leaned forward—"what would you do if one of those children was taken from you? Like Flora has been taken from her own father, and now Joel from his?"

Zeke swallowed hard and looked down at the dirt under his feet.

"Those helpless young ones in that cave are just as loved and just as precious as your own. Do you want to be the one to go home to Mr. Kimball and tell him we gave up? Will you go back with me to Cork to tell Mrs. Colfax we left her son with five of the worst men to grace this part of the country?"

Zeke looked up at his brother-in-law and the two seemed to have a silent conversation about their options. A shrug of a shoulder, a twitch of the lip, and the two men came to a decision.

"All right," Zeke said, nodding. "We'll stay."

Jacob was a little surprised at how easily he'd swung from one decision to another, but he didn't want to question it too hard for fear of changing the man's mind again.

"Okay, then. I still think the original plan is our best bet," Jacob said. "We can wait till one of those fellas is outside the cave and the others are inside, and take them out one at a time."

"Like an ambush?" Boyd asked.

"Exactly. As long as we stay out of sight from the mouth of the cave we should be just fine."

"They'll never guess what's coming," Zeke said, grinning now that he'd committed himself again—perhaps more so than before. "They're just grimy criminals. There's no way they will be able to beat us."

"Zeke," Jacob said seriously. "We can't underestimate these people. There's a reason they're still free and not rotting in a jail cell somewhere. We have to be smart about this."

"All right, then, what are we waiting for? Let's get to it so we can get home."

"Patience," Jacob said in a carrying whisper. But Zeke was already moving ahead and may not have heard him.

The three crept down the trail back toward where the enormous boulder would block the outlaws' view of their approach. Jacob strained to listen, to get a sense of what was going on just out of his view. It seemed too quiet to have more than maybe a couple of the outlaws outside the cave, but Jacob could smell the campfire burning down to embers.

"I don't hear anything," Zeke said excitedly. "We can get them now! The next one that comes outta there is gonna get a bullet in the side."

He strode on ahead, ignoring Jacob's hissing commands to wait and be careful. Zeke was making too much noise. Jacob couldn't reach him to pull him back before the other man popped his head and shoulders around the corner of the large stone wall. He moved into view of whoever might be at the campsite before he even had his pistol ready.

"Zeke!" Jacob whispered, desperate not to blow their cover.

A gunshot tore through the quiet.

Jacob started forward to help Zeke, but he was too slow. The man cried out, first in pain from the bullet piercing his upper arm, and then again from the pain of being seized and manhandled by the two outlaws who had been on guard.

"Who the hell is this?" one of the men asked angrily. "Where did you come from? You meddling sons-a-b—"

"Who else is out there?" the other man asked.

Jacob held his breath and backed away from the trail. He held Boyd back, flat against the boulder, watching as the grimy outlaw strode out from cover and into view. He looked right and left; he peered into the forest in front of him. With the hard afternoon light, the shadows between the trees were dark and distinct, hiding movement. As long as the man didn't come around to their side of the boulder, Jacob and Boyd would be safe.

Jacob readied his revolver, holding it steady, and aimed at the curve around which the outlaw might come.

After a few seconds of searching, the man returned back to the campsite, out of Jacob's line of sight.

"Grab that one," the voice commanded on the other side of the boulder. "If he's come after these two, there's more to their story than they're telling us."

"What are we doing with them? What if there's more of 'em?"

"Let's take 'em down to the depths of the mine. Maybe being down the shaft will jog their memory."

Jacob heard a series of pained cries as Flora, Joel, and Zeke were seized and likely dragged down into the dark, narrow cave. He could smell the fire outside the mouth of the entrance still burning, but try as he might he couldn't hear any human. The several pairs of footsteps faded away down the path and Jacob and Boyd were left alone.

"How can we get them now?" Boyd asked in a panicked whisper. "We have to go back to town. Get more men."

Jacob shook his head. There was still a way to do this. He just had to outthink the gang leader and stay one step ahead. They had to be quick about it, though. Before Zeke bled out. Before the men realized that Flora and Joel couldn't help them. With every moment that slipped by, the chance of getting all of their group safely back to Elk Springs grew smaller and smaller.

He and Boyd retreated to consider their options and make a plan.

"Jacob, we need to go back. We need to get help. We can't do this. There's too many of them. And too few of us. We can't. Jacob, we can't!"

"Come on now, Boyd," Jacob said soothingly. "Calm down now. If we take the time to go all the way back to town, who knows what will happen to them. Zeke's bleeding with every second we waste."

"Yeah, but—"

"It's too far. That's too much time. We have to figure this out on our own. Here. Now."

"Jacob, I don't know . . ."

"Do you want to go, then?"

Jacob gave the man a hard look. He needed to know if he was alone in this, if he would have to concoct a plan that was him against the entire outlaw gang, if he had any other kind of help on his side. Boyd swallowed under Jacob's gaze and looked down at his feet.

"I guess . . . I . . . yeah, okay. You're right. My sister will skin me alive if I come home without Zeke."

Working as quickly and quietly as they could, Jacob and Boyd spent the next fifteen minutes finalizing the plan for what would hopefully be their final assault. With all the tools they needed in hand, Jacob and Boyd headed back down the trail toward the cave for one final attempt at rescuing the captives.

It felt as though he was repeating himself—tentative attack only to be taken down before he even started. If this plan didn't work, Jacob despaired of ever rescuing the other three. He already worried about the innocent girl being in their clutches for too long, and what had happened to her in all the time Jacob couldn't see.

But he squared his shoulders and readied himself for the battle ahead.

Jacob cautiously rounded the corner, hugging the boulder with his back, and approached the mouth of the cave. With the heat of the afternoon, the group of outlaws had retreated into the cool of the cave. Sounds of their shouts, pickaxes, clanging, and arguing came echoing out of the narrow hole in the ground.

After he and Boyd had properly set up their plan, Jacob stepped to the opening of the cave and shouted:

"We've come to claim the bounty!"

CHAPTER THIRTEEN

Jacob stood in the mouth of the cave, knowing that he could be targeted and shot with no effort from his enemy. His entire frame would be backlit, his silhouette providing the exact target for the outlaws in the cave below.

"Bring out the outlaws—Flora Kimball and Joe Colfax," Jacob shouted again. "We'll be claiming their bounties. You have no right to them."

Boyd stood off to the side of the cave, shaking the trembles from his hands, as Jacob called for the dangerous men to show themselves.

"Stay out of sight," Jacob reminded him.

Deep down in the darkness of the cave, he heard the outlaws muttering to each other, probably debating the next step. It was always to Jacob's advantage when he came across a group with no clear leader. Their infighting would work in his favor.

"Go to hell!" a deep voice shouted up at him.

"I'm here for the three I know you have," Jacob yelled. "There's no use protecting them. They need to meet their justice."

More muttering and heated discussions floated up from the cave. Jacob pressed on loudly.

"The girl may have tricked you into thinking she's innocent, but the law says otherwise."

"If there's a bounty, we'll be the ones collecting," a voice shouted back to Jacob.

He grinned to himself. "Maybe we can come to some sort of agreement. I'd be happy to discuss it peaceably in the light of day."

He held both of his hands out, so by his silhouette it was clear he was not holding any weapons. If he could draw at least one of them out . . .

Before he had even finished the thought, Jacob heard footsteps echoing off the rock walls, getting ever louder as one of the men stalked out of the cave toward him. As he moved into the light, Jacob saw that he was the tall, bullying man the others had called Morris.

"Let's see those hands," Jacob said. "I'm not armed, and I don't want to negotiate with a man who is."

"Who said anything about negotiating?" the man asked with a snarl. He pointed his shotgun at Jacob, who kept his hands in the air. "You're gonna give us the details of that bounty. And then we're gonna leave here with the prisoners. Shoulda thought about that before you opened your big mouth."

"Wait, now." Jacob kept his hands in the air, signaling his innocence, but took a small step toward the man. Behind him, Boyd waited, eyes huge and fearful but still ready to play his part. "We can talk about this. How're y'all going to move three outlaws without horses?"

The other man's face grew dark. "What did you do with our horses?"

In a panic he turned to follow the trail to where their horses had been corralled, but Boyd was ready. Before the tall man had even finished his pivot, the other had swung down and hard with a shovel he had swiped from the outlaws' stash. The direct hit knocked the man unconscious immediately.

Morris collapsed into Boyd's arms and was

dragged away. Jacob did his best to disguise the silhouette of this interaction from whoever might be watching below, but now his window of opportunity was closing even faster.

"Morris?" a voice called up from below. "Where'd you go?"

"Your friend went to go check on the horses, since you have such a ride ahead of you."

Jacob glanced off to the side of the trail, pleased to see Boyd had already tied and gagged their first man. Cattle-rassling fast.

"Come on out, now. Bring the hostages with you. Their bounty will feed us for months."

After a beat of silence, the same voice called up again. "Where's Morris?"

Jacob glanced over. The man was still unconscious, Boyd grinning over him.

"He's busy. I told you. There's no point staying here any longer. By now you probably have figured out that this ain't a real gold mine, right?"

"Wait. How did you . . . ?"

"That's their scam." Jacob took a step farther into the cave. "That trio has bilked half a dozen people out of finder's fees and false maps by claiming they knew the way to a secret gold mine or silver mine. How much did the girl's story cost you?"

"Well, actually, we—"

Another voice: "Shut up!"

Jacob grinned to himself, imagining the men fighting down below, not paying attention, giving him a little more ground to press his advantage.

"That's why there's such a big bounty out for them." Jacob continued, pretending he hadn't heard their arguing. "And why I don't intend to leave this mountain without them."

There was one last pause before they shouted to him again.

"Go to hell! We're not giving anything up. Especially not if you have Morris."

"All right, then. I tried reasoning with you. I tried being nice. No more. You have ten seconds to come up out of there before I blow you out."

"Bull!"

"Let us go!" Flora cried.

Jacob felt a twinge of guilt. She didn't know him. She hadn't met him. And it was unlikely that either Zeke or Joel had had a chance to talk to her privately. For all the poor girl knew, he was just as dangerous as the men who currently held her captive. Out of the frying pan, into the fire.

"Are you going to save yourself and those

bounties you have tied up?" Jacob asked. "If you don't die immediately from the explosion, you're sentencing yourself to a long starvation or suffocation from the cave-in. Best come out now."

"I'm calling your bluff," Pickens said. "There's no way this girl is any kind of criminal."

Jacob took a deep breath, considering his next move. But he was out of maneuvers. This was the last thing he could do before he would either have to admit defeat for the first time or risk getting everyone killed.

He laughed. "Your funeral. Ten . . . nine . . . eight . . ."

As he counted down loudly, he moved to the side of the trail where, earlier, he'd planted the prop. It had to be convincing and it had to be ready in advance, in case negotiations had gotten to this step.

". . . five . . . four . . ."

Jacob turned his back to the mouth of the cave so the men inside were blocked from seeing what he did. The bundle of dried branches was bound tightly. It was small and narrow, as close to the dimensions of a stick of dynamite that Jacob could manage. With one longer branch sticking out of one end, in silhouette it resembled dynamite so closely that Jacob was the only one who should be able to tell the difference.

"... two ... one!"

Jacob held the end of the bundle over the still-smoldering campfire, waited for the spark to catch, and then tossed the smoking decoy down into the dark cave.

"Here it comes!" he shouted.

CHAPTER FOURTEEN

With every dangerous criminal that Jacob Payne hunted down, there would always be a small moment, a breath of time when he doubted himself, when the plan could collapse. A moment when he could fail. Immediately after he tossed the smoking bundle down into the cave, Jacob closed his eyes tightly and clenched his fists. That brief second to say a desperate prayer calmed his nerves.

He opened his eyes when he heard the yelps and cursing coming from the darkness. Jacob walked a few steps down into the mouth of the cave, closer to where his homemade smoke decoy was burning and hopefully forcing the outlaws out. Behind him, Boyd stood ready and waiting silently. The forest filled with the commotion, shuffling, and yelling as the sounds of his enemies bounced off the rock walls.

"Leave them!" one of the men yelled. "They're not worth it!"

"No!" Flora cried.

"Let us go!" Joel yelled.

It must be chaos down there, Jacob thought. He didn't know what kind of lantern or light source they had been working with, but as he couldn't see anything in the corridor ahead, it must not be much.

"Are they coming?" Boyd whispered.

Jacob nodded, drawing his gun. They would only have one chance to overpower the men as they exited the cave. He stepped backward back into the afternoon light.

"Come on!" one of the men shouted, getting closer.

Time slowed as the enemy approached.

When he was putting together the decoy dynamite, Jacob had thought carefully about how he could quickly capture five armed men, with only himself and Boyd to man the weapons. He could easily tie up one, probably two of the men on his own, but that left three for the inexperienced local to handle, and they couldn't depend on Joel or Zeke being able to help when the time came. There was no question that Jacob would need to be creative with this step in his plan.

He had thought about it, weighed his options, and considered what assets he had at his disposal. Once he took a wider view of the whole situation, Jacob realized he had much more to work with than just the one man at his side.

Now, as he waited on edge for the four remaining dangerous outlaws to all exit the cave, Jacob stepped back to the side, his back against the boulder wall, squatted down, and picked up the end of the rope that he had previously left lying there in the dirt. The length of the rope was limp on the ground, across the mouth of the cave, until it curved up, the other end was securely tied to the saddle of his horse, Blaze.

The strength and control of that mustang was an ace up his sleeve that Jacob had completely forgotten he'd had. He supposed he'd gotten too used to the absence of Paint—especially after having to disregard Franny entirely. He was newly encouraged when he remembered that Blaze, or maybe the other horses, could be brought in to help.

As the men poured out of the cave, Jacob pulled up his end of the rope. Pickens and his cohorts were too frantic and panicked to be paying close-enough attention, and the low rope tripped every single one of them. They fell, one after another getting caught, ankles twisting, knees buckling. The fourth one out of the cave fell fastest, over his own feet and into the back of Pickens. One man grabbed at another to hold him up, and they ended up with elbows and arms enmeshed, crashing to the ground. One after another, the men fell over each other into a tangled mess in the dirt.

Jacob and Boyd lost no time in pushing their advantage.

The shortest of the men scrambled to his feet first, but fumbled in drawing his weapon. Boyd rushed forward with a large stone in one hand and his pistol in the other. Pickens, sprawled in the dirt, grabbed for Boyd's feet as he passed, tripping him. But Boyd kept his feet under him and reached the short man. He swung down, hard and fast, smashing his stone into the side of the man's head and incapacitating him. The man crumpled on the ground and Boyd turned to take on another.

While Boyd was taking care of that man, Jacob grabbed the end of the rope. Leaving it still tied to Blaze's saddle, he wrapped his end three times quickly around the outlaw with the big black beard before he was able to climb to his feet. The man kicked out at Jacob and spat at him.

"You son of a—!"

Jacob kicked the man in the ribs, knocking the wind out of him before he could finish his angry cursing. He pulled a sweaty handkerchief out of his pocket and stuffed it in the man's mouth, further silencing him.

As he finished tying the knot, Jacob heard a *crack* behind him and in front of him almost simultaneously and looked around the space. Pickens had climbed to his feet and pulled his weapon, turning it on Jacob and firing. Whether because of his aim or because of Jacob's movement, the shot missed, hitting the stone wall behind him and breaking a chunk off the boulder.

Pickens saw that Jacob had noticed where the bullet came from and grinned at him. With two teeth missing on the right side of his mouth, the man looked manic. Jacob was a quick draw, but had not yet had a chance to pull his revolver when Pickens collapsed into the dirt. As he crumpled, Boyd's form with a now-bloody stone held in one hand loomed behind.

The fourth and final outlaw had not even stuck around to try to fight it out. He had taken longer to get to his feet, but now was racing as fast as he could down the mountain, off the trail and toward the woods where Jacob had watched their group before. The outlaw must have been injured in his fall; he seemed to be cautious about putting weight on his right foot.

Jacob hesitated only a moment before darting off after him. The man was still close enough that he could have gotten off a clean shot and stopped his progress. Instead, Jacob bounded off down the mountain, catching up with the man in seconds and tackling him to the ground.

The outlaw fought back, kicking, punching, and trying to bite Jacob when his arm got close enough. They tussled in the dirt for a tense ten seconds before Jacob's muscular legs gave him the advantage. He had the other man pinned in the dirt, each of Jacob's legs pinning an arm down, and the outlaw squirmed underneath.

"You want to give up now?" Jacob asked. "Make this easy on yourself? Or do I have to knock you out?"

"You best kill me," the man hissed.

Jacob smirked. "Oh no, my friend. I won't be denying the law their due."

He pulled his fist back, kneeling hard on the man's arms to hold him in place, and swung.

Jacob's knuckles connected directly with the man's jaw, just below his ear, knocking him unconscious and leaving him limp in the dirt.

Jacob let out a long, slow breath. Against all odds, they had managed to subdue five outlaws without killing any of them. Jacob had to keep reminding himself that one of these days he would have no choice, that he would have to kill a fugitive to protect himself or someone else. But he was grateful today was not that day.

Fortunately the man was not all that large. Even with his dead weight, Jacob was able to heft him over his shoulder and carry him back up the incline toward the campsite and the others.

The unconscious outlaw dumped alongside the first, Jacob crossed the dirt campsite to where Pickens lay collapsed. There was a tiny rivulet of blood trailing down the back of his head into the dirt, but when Jacob looked closely and probed a bit with his fingers, he decided the cut was shallow and the man would be fine.

Jacob lifted the man to his feet, holding him upright under the armpits. As he was unconscious, the dead weight was difficult to maneuver, but with Boyd's help he managed to get the man up onto the horse, tied and fixed in place.

One by one each of the incapacitated outlaws was trussed up and planted on top of a horse. Jacob had lied, of course—the outlaws' horses were here the whole time.

Jacob surveyed his and Boyd's handiwork, satisfied. Each of these men was complicit in a kidnapping at the very least. But Jacob knew the type—it was likely they were involved in deeper, more dangerous plots. He would take them all back to Elk Springs and let Sheriff Dale deal with them. They could be installed safely in the town jail while wires went out to other towns in the area once they were up and running again.

Once the group of men were subdued securely, it only took a few minutes to hike down into the cave, untie Joel, Zeke, and Flora, and make the necessary explanations. The poor prisoners had had a few petrifying moments, of course, waiting for the "dynamite" to blow up and end them, but they'd soon realized that the burning and smoke was coming from something other than explosive.

"And then once we realized it was just a decoy, it just became a matter of staying out of your way until the rest of your plan had unfolded," Zeke concluded.

Flora was eager to get home, and they still

had just enough light left in the day to make it back to her family's farm. Joel led the entire caravan back down the mountain trail.

They had left Flora untethered to a criminal. She had protested, insisting she could do her part to guard them, until Jacob pointed out that she was unarmed. Being free of that burden, Flora rode up at the front of the caravan, side by side with Joel. Jacob was too far back to hear what they said to each other, but the grins they traded back and forth said plenty.

CHAPTER FIFTEEN

Just as dusk began to settle, Joel led them through the gap in the fence on the backside of the Kimball farm. Flora trotted on ahead, eager to see her family again.

Once Jacob, Boyd, and Zeke had secured their prisoners and their horses by the fence at the front of the property, Jacob approached where Joel was talking to Kimball out on the front porch.

"Sir? Mr. Kimball? I'd . . ." Joel looked at Flora with an expression of worship. "I'd like to marry your daughter."

"I know he's not of our faith, Father," Flora said quickly, "but he's a good man and he loves me and I'm not sure, now, that—"

"Hush, child," Kimball said gently, putting

his large, rough hand on his daughter's cheek. "You don't have to explain anything to me. Your mother and I had despaired of ever finding a man of our Heavenly Father worthy of you, anyway. And now, with this whole adventure and the way people talk, I thought . . ." He trailed off and grew quiet.

Joel reached over and clasped Flora's hand. They presented a united front to her father, both wanting nothing more than to just be together, no matter what other circumstances may have led to it.

"I can't promise you it will be easy," Kimball said to them, coming out of his reverie. "The folks in this town have mighty strong opinions about us already, Flora. And now they have an opportunity to question your honor. Marrying Joel won't stop their wagging tongues."

"I know, Father. But I wanted to be his wife a week ago, and even more so now. Please say we have your blessing."

There was another long pause as Kimball looked over the pair. Finally he addressed his proclamation to Joel.

"Son," he said, offering his hand. "You've begun this marriage protecting my daughter at risk of your own life. I expect you to continue the same level of love and protection for the rest of it."

"Yes, sir. Of course, sir. I'm happy to." Joel shook his new father-in-law's hand vigorously, unable to keep the wide grin from his face. "Can we get married today?"

Kimball chuckled. "Your mother would kill me if I let you get married without her being here. We'll send them word. I promise it will be soon."

Jacob wasn't sure the boy had heard, though. He had already turned to his bride-to-be and taken her in his arms. Jacob tried not to watch, to give them a little privacy. But it was clear from what he did see that Joel and Flora would never be happier with anyone else. This was as sure an example of everything working together for good as Jacob would ever see.

The two lovebirds soon hurried into the house. Flora had been wearing the same dress for several days, and they both needed something more substantial in their stomach than simply jerky.

"I'll see to it that word is sent to his parents on my way back through Elk Springs," Jacob promised. "Assuming the wire is fixed by now."

"I appreciate that," Kimball said. "Joel's parents were our closest friends when they lived here, and though I wish the circumstances could be different, I'm sure those two will make a happy couple."

"You ready to go back to town now?" Zeke asked, walking up.

Jacob looked up to where Boyd was standing guard over their prisoners. Each of the five men wore an expression of anger and disappointment. Whatever big plans they had had for the rumored Herron Gold Mine, they'd have to rethink that completely.

"That reminds me," Kimball said, following Jacob's gaze. "While you were gone Reverend Fowler came back with news from Tucson. Homer Pickens is wanted for bank robbery. There's a bounty of three hundred dollars on his head."

Zeke let out a low whistle. "Three hundred? Must have been some robbery."

Kimball continued. "And judging from the descriptions the reverend gave me, I would bet these others you've captured are members of the Slippery Stone Gang that has been roaming these mountains."

"I thought that gang was up in Prescott," Jacob said.

"Some are." Kimball nodded. "But Stone likes to keep lawmen on their toes. He has so many men willing to kill and rob for him that he can split them up for different jobs."

"Well, ain't that a pleasant thought," Jacob said darkly.

"Exactly," Kimball agreed. "But that does mean that there's probably a bounty on those men, too. They could have been anywhere in the Arizona Territory wreaking havoc. You all should be sure to check in with the sheriff and see what can be salvaged from this adventure."

Excitement was dawning on Zeke's face. He looked back at Boyd, who remained focused, his revolver pointed at the prisoners.

"A few hundred dollars split between us is good money," Zeke said. "We're ready as soon as you are, Jacob."

"You boys go ahead," Jacob told him. He walked to the horses alongside Zeke. "We didn't know there would be a bounty when we set off, and I know you all risked more than I did. You take these men back to town and the sheriff will see to your reward. Any man who would risk so much for a neighbor in face of such adversity deserves whatever the world will gift him."

Boyd and Zeke exchanged a glance before nodding, accepting what Jacob had offered them.

"Thank you kindly, Jacob," Zeke said,

offering a shake with his uninjured arm. "We appreciate what you've done for Elk Springs and for both of us. A good man like you doesn't come along all the time, but know that you're always welcome here."

"I know my Sarah would be happy to host you any time," Boyd added.

"I appreciate that. I really do. Next time I'm on this side of the territory I'll take you up on it."

"All right, then," Zeke said as he mounted his horse. "We'll be seeing you, Jacob."

Both men tipped their hats and began the ride back to Elk Springs, a line of five tied outlaws riding between them.

"I couldn't help overhearing," Kimball said, as Jacob turned back toward the farmhouse. "That's very generous of you to let those men claim the reward when you did so much of the work."

Jacob shrugged. "There will be more rewards. This was supposed to be a break from that work, anyway."

Kimball chuckled. "Guess it didn't work out the way you planned."

"No, sir, it didn't."

"What do you think you'll do now?"

Jacob shrugged again. "The horse I'm riding

is just a loan. I've got to take Franny back to her owner soon, so I guess I'll just make my way back to Tucson now. There's bound to be a new report ready."

"Those outlaws never stop."

"No, they don't."

Jacob was about to head into the barn to get Franny saddled and ready to head back down the mountain, when Kimball stopped him.

"I've been thinking. The whole time you were gone, putting yourself at risk for my daughter, I was wondering what I could do to ever repay you."

"There's no need—"

"Hush, now." Kimball fixed him with a hard stare. "There is a need. Flora is dearer to me than you may realize. With her blessed mother gone, and us moved all the way out to Arizona, Flora and Edith are the only things left that are around to remind me of the love of my youth. When you went after her, I was left with hours imagining what I would do if you didn't succeed."

Jacob listened respectfully, thinking of his own memory of his marriage, and the little he had left of his late wife.

"There is nothing that can make up for what you've given back to me, but I thought maybe you'd accept a small gift of my appreciation."

Jacob smiled. "I will, sir. Something small I can take with me back to Tucson would be kind and much appreciated."

"Wonderful." Kimball beamed. "I hoped you'd say that. Come with me."

Jacob moved to follow the older man into the house, but instead he turned the opposite direction to lead him out into the pasture. Jacob was confused. Maybe it was something that had fallen out of his pocket, or a little medallion he kept pinned to a fence somewhere. Kimball walked through the grass with Jacob trailing behind him, evidently with a destination in mind.

"Here we are," Kimball said proudly, far sooner than Jacob expected.

Jacob looked around. "Is it . . . I'm sorry, sir, but if you meant to get something from Blaze's saddlebags I think those are already in your house."

"No, no. Not the saddlebags. I want you to have Blaze."

"A horse? No, I—"

"You already agreed to take the gift," Kimball said with a teasing glint in his eye. "You can't let me down now, son."

"Aw, now, don't put it like that." Jacob backed up a couple steps. The truth was, he and Blaze had bonded more quickly than any of the other horses he had looked at since his own was shot. If he had been forced to go after that wild gang with Bonnie's horse, who knew what kind of disaster might have struck. Jacob already loved Blaze, and did indeed want to take him home. But surely this was too much. "Don't you need him?"

Kimball smiled. "Not hardly. With all the young ones around, he doesn't get near enough exercise. You'd be doing both me and Blaze a favor. He's a mustang, Jacob. Teaming up with a man like you would be the best thing for him."

"Well, but . . ." Jacob dithered. "At least let me buy him from you, Mr. Kimball. I got a sack of cash in my bag that's just been waiting till I found the right horse to invest in. I wouldn't feel right taking such a gorgeous creature free of charge."

"It's not free of charge, Jacob Payne." Kimball gently punched Jacob in the arm. "Didn't I tell you I offered a bounty on any man who could bring my daughter back safe and sound to me?"

"You did not." Jacob grinned in spite of himself.

"Sure, I did. Exactly the cost of one mustang named Blaze. Although, I suppose now that he's yours you can change his name if you see fit."

"I wouldn't change such a fine name for a fine horse."

"Ah-ha!" Kimball said triumphantly. "You admit you're going to accept him."

"I mean, I—"

"Give an old man like me something, Jacob. The best way I know to protect my daughter is to provide for the man who did. Blaze is yours."

Jacob let out a slow breath before nodding. "All right, Mr. Kimball. I . . . I won't fight you. Blaze will come home with me."

"And if you do come back up to Elk Springs, be sure to send word out here so I can come see him."

"Will do, sir."

When Jacob comes across a family that has fallen victim to horse thieves, he can't just ride on and leave them to his fate. He's not yet a bounty hunter, but Jacob Payne can still hunt down the evil-doers. Tucson will be waiting for him once he brings these men to justice.

Sign-up to download this prequel story for free from my website: **http://atbutler.com/jp-free**

ALSO BY A.T. BUTLER

Jacob Payne, Bounty Hunter Series:

Trouble By Any Name

Danger in the Canyon

Justice for Jasper

Blood on the Mountain

Outlaw Country

Death By Grit

Desert Rage

Arizona Legacy

Fool's Demise

Silent Night

Courage on the Oregon Trail Series:

Westward Courage

Faithful Trail

Frontier Sisters

Unyielding Heart

Wild Promise

Novels by A.T. Butler:

Jacob Payne, a bounty hunter in the Arizona Territory, heard the altercation in the crowded saloon before he saw it.

He crossed the threshold into the Golden Saddle Saloon in Tucson, and let his eyes adjust to the dim light. On the right side of the room, nearest where he walked in, the bar was packed with men elbowing each other for space. A half dozen of Holly Merritt's girls squeezed in between, entertaining their guests and helping them drink all the beer that the bartender could serve. The bright colors on the women stood out against the dirty leather of the men and Jacob smiled to himself to think about how each one of those men planned to end their night.

It was a Saturday, and it seemed as though every person in Tucson was in the saloon trying to fit in as much sinning as possible before the Lord's day the following morning. Past the bar, throughout the rest of the room, tables were crowded with men playing poker, drinking, grabbing at passing women, laughing and telling stories.

But on the far side of the room, back where the gamblers Lucky and Abe had virtually been living for the last couple of weeks as they took all the other men's money, a shoving match had broken out.

"I'll show you—" an angry voice called above the noise.

Jacob pushed through the crowd to get to the skirmish before it could spread. His broad shoulders and more than six feet of height made him a formidable force; men saw him coming and got out of the way. In a few purposeful strides, he had reached the brawling gamblers. He hesitated, and in that split second a short and stocky, but fit, red-headed man Jacob didn't recognize landed a punch right to Lucky's cheekbone.

"You son-of-a—" Abe yelled as he pushed the short man back.

Jacob stepped in between them, and put his

hands up to ward off the gambler. In spite of the shorter man's hit, two on one would never be a fair fight.

"Hold on here," he said.

"What's all this?" a deep, gravelly voice asked angrily.

Randall Hall, the owner of the saloon, glared at Jacob. "You causing trouble in my establishment, Payne?"

Randall stood up to his full height. Though several inches shorter than Jacob, Randall wielded his wide barrel chest, taking up as much room as he could as he asserted his authority. Holly Merritt waited just behind him, her warm brown curls piled on top of her head, and a gold shawl pulled tightly around her. She surveyed the damage to the saloon with an anxious look.

"No, sir," Jacob answered patiently.

Before he could explain any further, the short man Jacob had intended to be protecting knocked into him from behind as he made to go after Lucky again.

"Hey!" Jacob said.

He stumbled to his left; the unknown man threw himself at the gambler, pummeling him in the ribs with punch after punch.

"That's enough," Randall said, grabbing for the shorter man.

Jacob regained his footing and again stepped between the brawlers. This time, with Randall's help to hold the one back, they succeeded in ending the fight.

"What is this all about?" Randall asked, severely. "Mr. Timson, I would never have thought a man of your profession and class could be involved in a common barroom fistfight."

"What did you boys do to him?" Jacob asked the gamblers.

"Nothing," Lucky said indignantly, shaking off Jacob's grip.

The bounty hunter was almost inclined to believe him, seeing as that denial was literally the only word he had heard the man say in the several weeks he had been in Tucson.

"You did, you cheating snake," Timson sputtered. He writhed in Randall's grasp, trying and failing to break free from the man almost twice his weight.

"Is that true?" Jacob asked.

Lucky glared at him but Abe held Jacob's gaze. The gambler spit a long stream into a nearby spittoon before answering with a sly smile.

"We simply used our considerable skill at cards to relieve this man of some of his paper.

Really, we're doing him a favor. Less weight to move when he inevitably leaves town." The gambler grinned mockingly at Timson, wide enough that Jacob noticed he had a gold tooth on one side.

Jacob shook his head and sighed. "Come on, Abe. We both know what you're capable of. Did you cheat?" Jacob's eyes darted over the man, looking for a sign he was hiding cards, but saw nothing out of place. He glanced to the table, where the cards were still strewn about after the last hand. He raked over the edge of the poker table, and even underneath, looking for a mirror or any other clue.

Lucky and Abe had been playing in Tucson for weeks, and though they had been accused of cheating many times, none of the other men had been able to prove it. Jacob was beginning to think they really were just extremely talented players.

As he looked over the men, he noticed the crowd that was gathered around, watching them. Most of the saloon's patrons had lost interest once the fight had been broken up, but two men continued to watch. The taller one, thin as a rail but taller than Jacob, leaned against the back wall, biting the nails on his filthy left hand and pushing back his stringy dark hair as he took in the scene. The other, a blond, was as average-looking a man as Jacob had ever seen, but wore distinctive moss green cowboy boots. His face remained passive, and he hovered just behind Holly while he listened. Jacob had never seen these two strangers before and at least three dozen questions and suspicions popped into his mind.

He filed all these details away, just in case, but forced himself to stay focused on the situation at hand.

"I can't have any more disturbances in here, boys," Holly said with a teasing lilt. "Ruins the mood, you know."

She caught Jacob watching her and winked. Though he had never personally been a customer of Holly's, they had always had an easy repartee. He respected the way she ran her business, and she respected the way he did his own work.

Timson's chest still heaved as he caught his breath again. His anger seemed to be abating.

"Just give me back my money, fellas, and we'll forget all about this."

"Not a chance," Abe said.

Instead of responding with words, Lucky simply glared and left the mob gathered. He pushed through the crowd and Jacob lost sight of him.

Randall moved to follow, but Timson stopped him.

"Let him go. It's this other one that actually has the cash. I saw him scoop it up when I first pushed his friend. Whatever it is they're doing, they're in this together. I just want my money."

Timson reached into his coat pocket and pulled out his billfold. Jacob couldn't help but notice it had a small red rose embroidered in the corner of the leather. He had never seen another billfold like it, either here in the territory, or back when he lived in Virginia.

"You're not from around here, are you?" he asked.

Timson looked at him in surprise and shook his head. "No. Just passing through. I come from Boston, by way of about three dozen smaller cities between there and here."

Before he could explain any further, the conversation was interrupted yet again by a familiar voice.

"Jacob Payne, why do I always find you in the middle of trouble?"

I grew up in the southwest—California Missions, snakes and constant threat of drought weaving the backdrop of my childhood.

But it wasn't until I moved to Texas a few years ago that the magic and mythology of the American West began to seep into my soul.

I'd love to write about Jacob Payne for a long time. ...

If you enjoyed this book, a review on your favorite retailer would be greatly appreciated.

Be sure to sign up for my newsletter for all the updates on future books.

- A